DOGGY BAG

DOGGY BAG

RONALD SUKENICK

for
Hagerasi
enjoy
Ron Sukenick

BLACK ICE
BOOKS

BOULDER • NORMAL

First edition
First printing 1994

Published by Fiction Collective Two with support given by the English Department Publications Unit of Illinois State University, the English Department Publications Center of the University of Colorado at Boulder, and the Illinois Arts Council

Address all inquiries to: Fiction Collective Two, c/o English Department, Publications Center, Campus Box 494, University of Colorado at Boulder, Boulder, CO 80309-0494

Credits:
"Who Are These People?" *Fiction International*; "Name of the Dog," *Boulevard*; "Doggy Bag," *Central Park*; "A Mummy's Curse," *New Novel Review*; "50,010,008," *To*; "The Wondering Jew and the Black Widow Murders, or the Return of the Planet of the Apes," *Southern Plains Review*; "The Burial of Count Orgasm," *The Iowa Review*; "Death on the Supply Side," *Talus*

Thanks to the Council on Research and Creative Work, University of Colorado, for its support

Doggy Bag
Ronald Sukenick

ISBN: Paper, 0-932511-82-1, $7.00

Produced and printed in the United States of America

Cover Design: Dave LeFleur

for my
French Frey

who are these people?}-->

name of the dog}==>

doggy bag}#########################::::::::::::::------------->

a mummy's curse}*************************+++++++++===--->

50,010,008}}}}}}}}}}}}}}}))))))>>>>>////////%%%%%%%%::::===>

the wondering jew and the black widow murders, or the
return of the planet of the apes}"""""""""""" ' ' ' ' '~~~~~~~~~---->

the burial of count orgasm}|||||||||||::::::::...... . . . . .

death on the supply side}_______________--------------~~~~~~~~~~

who are these people?}------------------>

I'm standing on line waiting to get into the Uffizi, but this is an understatement. I'm heading for the Uffizi yesterday in a leisurely way, expecting to "do" it, as Henry James might say, for the third time after a lapse of twenty-odd years, when as my "companion," as Henry James might call her, and myself turn into the piazza in front of the entrance, I lower my eyes from the huge imposition of the Palazzo della Signoria, the calculated imbalance of the tower implying that matter can always crush us, and whose rough elegance never fails to bowl me over, and behold a swarm of people in front of the museum. It takes me almost a minute to register what my eyes already see, which is that the crowd is actually a line, starting at the entrance to the museum, and snaking back through the piazza in many bends contained by crowd control fences and then beyond extending well toward the Arno for the length of several city blocks.

Thinking this situation is probably the result of some unfortunate coincidence of tour groups, my "companion" and I go to a cafe and come back in three quarters of an hour. The line is still longer. I ask a guard how long the wait will be and he tells me, casually, as if it were not a very busy day, "An hour or so." I wait a bit to see if the line will get shorter. It gets longer. I ask the guard when the best time to come might be. He says, "You come a half hour before the museum opens, you go right in."

So it's eight-thirty in the morning and I'm standing on line waiting to get into the Uffizi when it opens at nine. The line is a mere, I would say, two blocks long. This may be an improvement over yesterday, but for one used to breezing into the Uffizi in the past, then breezing out for a cup of coffee and back in for another look at those Botticellis or maybe a Duccio that caught my eye this time, it's still a bit bizarre.

My "companion," who has never been through the Uffizi, is simultaneously eager and wondering whether it's worth the effort.

"It's worth it," I tell her. And it is for my "companion." Whether it is for me, and if so, how, is another story. This one.

I look around at this morning's mob, sleepy at so early an hour, but sullenly determined to push on with the tourist-work. I flash on an ancient *New Yorker* cartoon of a wealthy snob couple looking appalled at the crowds in an air terminal, the old gent quoted in the caption saying, "Who *are* these people?"

My "companion" strikes up a conversation with a girl from Yale. A girl from Yale? Yes. A Black girl from Yale. When I was an undergrad not so long ago, Jewish males had a hard time getting into Yale, even in very limited numbers. Catholic boys probably didn't find it too easy either, and then only if they were white. Whether that would have included Italians by Yale definitions of the time I'm not sure.

"Bet they open a half hour late too," says a sleepy boy behind me. "You staying at the hostel? Oh," he says as I turn around. "Sorry. Most people seem to be."

He's wearing sandals, Bermuda shorts, a T-shirt that says "Alternative Tentacles," and a knapsack.

"You mind the wait?" I ask.

"Not really. Last year I waited twelve hours to hear Sonic Youth," responds my "interlocutor," as Henry James might call him.

A lot, if not most of the crowd on line could be staying at the hostel it appears as I look around. And at least two thirds of the tourist horde seem to be Americans.

"Our tour got right in the Academy yesterday," says an

older man next to the kid. He's wearing a white T-shirt with buttons at the collar that articulates a lot of flab and a webbed red baseball cap, owns a hardware store in Peoria or something. "First thing we see in there is this huge statue, you know, Michelangelo's 'David.' I says to myself, 'Sheez, if that's David, imagine what Goliath must look like.' Got some good shots though."

This guy is carrying a big VCR on his shoulder, looks like it weighs five pounds. Eight-thirty in the morning and he's already sweating. Used to be you could get away with a little Brownie for snapshots, now you got to lug around this big TV camera item to get it all in moving color. The tourist-work is getting harder, the tourist-duty more demanding, as the American Century rolls on.

"Yeah, I'm getting some good stuff. Wife just died of cancer. It's for her in a way."

"What do you mean by that, Harold?" asks a pale, potato-shaped blond girl.

"I guess I don't exactly know what I mean by that," says Harold.

"They had great post cards in the Academy," says the blond girl. "I like the one with the baby. I bought like three of those."

Meanwhile I get to talking to a young Italian woman who must be the only native on line and her excuse, judging by the sketch pad under her arm, is that she's an art student. She's wearing a pair of tight jeans and a loose T-shirt that says "Downie Duck" on the back and "New Yorks Tiger Base Balls" across the front. That's what it says. When I say I'm talking to her I'm exaggerating a bit, since she speaks minimal English and I minimal Italian, though it turns out we both know a little Spanish. In fact what we're doing is sort of making faces at one another and flailing our arms about, while uttering ejaculations in some weird polyglot. She looks at me, looks around at the intestinally queued line, looks up at the sky, and says something that sounds like "Giambozziallonі!" Whereupon I respond by putting my arms out palms up and turn down the corners of my mouth, saying something like, "Non c'e raggione," which I hope will indicate something like, "Beats me."

"Da dove lei?" she points at me. "Que pais you come? New York?"

I notice as she gestures in the direction of the Atlantic that one loose breast nipples her T-shirt in the *e* of "New" and the other in the *e* of "Tiger." E – E. Eeee.

"Si. You viene Firenze?"

She shakes her finger at me. "No, no. Firenze they no ama tourist."

"You're a tourist?" I misinterpret.

"No, no ama tourist."

"You no ama tourist." I point at my chest. "Am a tourist."

"No, no. How you say. No like tourist. In Firenze they bring dogs to tourist parts to go to bathroom."

"Ah?" So that explains dog shit city.

She waves her arm toward the line. "Flakes," she says contemptuously.

"You seen the candy palace yet?" asks the kid behind me.

"What's the candy palace?"

"*They* call it the Domo."

"The Duomo," says Harold. "I climbed up the top yesterday. Sheez that was hard work. Got some good shots though."

"This's my second time through this place," says the kid. "Went through yesterday. Probably go through again tomorrow."

It's nine o'clock and nothing is happening. If anything the line ahead seems to be getting longer. That's probably because newcomers keep discovering and joining friends and acquaintances toward the beginning of the line, or even people they vaguely recognize, people who in some cases don't appear to recognize them. If you say something about it they just answer, "She was saving my place," or "It's all right he's my boyfriend," or "I just went to the bathroom," or "This is where I was yesterday." The result is that even when the doors open punctually at nine the line grows faster than it advances.

After a while the kid in front of me says, "Hey, save my place, woodja, I'm gonna split over to the Bargello for an hour. Want me to bring you back a pizza?"

"Okay, no thanks," I tell him as he splits.

My "companion" is now flirting with some good-looking Italian guy who stops to ask her if she knows his uncle in San Francisco. "This is Nicolá," she tells me. "He has an uncle in San Francisco."

"Save my place," I tell her. "I'm going to get us some coffee." I invite the Italian girl along. Ee-ee. As we start drinking cappucinos at the bar of a nearby cafe I ask her if she doesn't mind the invasions of Americans.

"No, no," she says. "They bring soldi." She rubs her thumb back and forth across her index and middle fingers. "You know? Dinero. Bucks. Only problem, Americans are dirty, excuse I say it. And brutto. Stupid. Flakes. Who Michelangelo? who Da Vinci? Botticelli not spaghetti. Why you no wash in your country? And slow. And how you say, not efficient. And make lousy machine which no work."

"You're an artist?" I ask, pointing at her sketch pad.

She laughs, rather contemptuously it appears. "No, no,"

she shakes her finger. "I publicity. Study advertise in Uffizi. Look at stupid old pictures for new ideas. Everybody tired of all that," she waves toward the museum. Ee-ee.

We go back toward the line, the Italian girl telling me how Americans have no style. Turns out she's from Milano. I suppose from the point of view of Milan nothing else looks like it has any style. Everything in Milan has so much style it makes the Cinquecento seem almost homely. If in the architecture of the Palazzo della Signoria you can see the genius of design struggling with the brute strength of matter, the shape of a Milan-designed couch or lamp or car or even dress seems to suggest that matter doesn't matter any more. And in the high tech world of our fin-de-siècle maybe it doesn't, neither inert nor corporeal matter, yet if it doesn't what does and you remember that Milan was the home of the Futurists who dissolved matter in action and were early Fascists speeding with their Mussolini locomotives toward the Hitler death camps.

Loco motives. Why are we here? This is the mystery of the tourist-work. What are we after? This time around, it will turn out once I complete the Florence-work, Botticelli will seem too cute, even slick, and Donatello a little fey, but in the face of a Christ by da Vinci you may find matter struggling with itself on the verge of dissolution and transfiguration, a transfiguration without which matter remains merely matter, inert. I glance at the Italian girl whose breasts are jouncing under her T-shirt in the tradition of "Nude Descending a Stair Case." Ee-ee. Why is she more than meat?

Loco motives. Our needs are not rational, nor are our satisfactions. This is implicit in the tourist-work, the *opera*. In Italian the "work" is the *opera,* according to my dictionary. It is not yet the grand opera. But go from there.

I get back to the line, which now extends from the door of the Uffizi through the piazza to the road along the Arno and around the corner out of view. From there it goes all the way back to the Duomo and then to multiple pensione and hotels then to the youth hostel in the hills. From the hostel it actually snakes around to the airport and then onto a charter flight to Peoria, which is now the staging area for admission to the Uffizi since the line has gotten too long for the Italian peninsula. One tourist, backed up all the way to San Diego, is interviewed by a local newspaper wanting to know what she expects to find in the Uffizi. "I don't know," she says. "That's why we're going. We know it must be there, but we don't know what it is."

Luckily my "companion" is holding my place near the head of the line, still chatting with Nicola about his uncle in San Francisco. The kid back from the Bargello tells her "interlocutor," as Henry James might call him, that today is his second time through the Uffizi. "And tomorrow will be my third. Unless I manage to go again between now and then. You've probably seen it lots of times."

"Uffizi, niente," says Nicola. "Uffizi is for tourists. How many times you went to Disneyland?"

It's now well past noon and the line ahead is still getting longer. Everybody is beginning to realize that we are going to have to wait on line overnight if we're serious about seeing the Uffizi. A good-looking young woman with a knapsack asks if she can unroll her sleeping bag in front of me on line. The tourists behind me have already unloaded their packs and sleeping bags as far as the eye can see. Some have even pitched tents and started fires. So I say sure, what the hell, especially since she's so good looking. She's wearing one of those cut-off sweat shirts with armholes up to the boobs. This is particularly convenient since my "companion" says she wants to make a quick trip with Nicola to Rome so she can see the Coliseum by the light of the full moon. I warn her that the mosquitoes are dangerous but Nicola says that the muggers and rapists have killed all the mosquitoes, or at least that's what I understand him to say.

The girl with the armholes tells me that she's just been reading the *International Herald Tribune* and the Pope has persuaded Kurt Waldheim at their meeting in the Vatican to resign as President of Austria and take a job as coachman of one of Florence's horse-drawn tourist carriages so that he can meditate on the Uffizi's art treasures and renew his commitment to humanity. She says he's changed his name to Hurt Waldheim and that he beats his horse nearly to death and that the only reason he doesn't beat it completely to death is that he doesn't want to be accused of beating a dead horse. As she talks I notice through her armhole that she has two baby rabbits cradled between her breasts.

What happened in the Coliseum that night can never be re-experienced or described adequately or maybe even described at all. It can only be noted that it happened and has to be left at that. It began as an apparently foolish, even slapstick prank that turned on taking shots at the multitude of stray, starving and diseased cats that prowl the arena, but quickly escalated into an assault with a sledge hammer on Michelangelo's *Pieta* in St. Peter's that crushed the face of the Virgin. Among the other activities of that night about which we have accounts are the torture of small animals, the mocking of bag ladies and the ignoring of infants as they gag and scream and turn blue. I only knew about this because I was told about it by my "companion" and her "interlocutor" when they returned the next morning pale and sick. Much of what happened they didn't see and much of what they saw they couldn't talk about. Not without retching, if at all.

I'm not religious but I find that I do believe in what I would call sins against humanity. This phenomenon resembles that of crimes against humanity, and though it doesn't have the enormity of the latter partakes nonetheless of its absoluteness in the moral dimension. And as with crimes against humanity, sins against humanity are humanly unforgivable in that they can't be forgiven even if we should wish to do so. It is this absolute aspect of the spirit, once so well-represented in grand opera, that seems to be missing from the way we go about things.

This morning the young woman with the large armholes is forlorn. Her two rabbits have died. It seems that she crushed them while she slept. She says she should have known that she couldn't keep them alive under the circumstances. She says she read in the *International Herald Tribune* that pandas are doomed to disappear from the face of the earth.

I tell her that pandas are doomed to extinction because of the way we live. I tell her that everybody knows this.

The line starts moving now, slowly, into the Uffizi. The tourists are wistfully eager to begin their work. They're looking for something, but they don't know what it is.

k n o w w h a t i t i s

h a t i t i s

i t i s

i s

?

t h e

t h e t e x t

t h e t e x t o f l i f e

name of the dog}=====================================>

Strange logics dictate the text of life. The first time I travelled to Europe, thirty-five years ago, the very first person I met on European soil was Federico Fellini. I was an admirer of his early films, among which *La Strada* had already made him famous in the States, but I did not yet know that his work was to become a major sanction for my own, because he had not yet produced *Eight and a Half.*

I had come over on the Queen Elizabeth. Five days in tourist class in the hothouse milieu of a giant ocean liner is something like being in summer camp. People you've never seen before become the target of feelings more intense than those aroused by close family members. There's something moving about such a voyage, possibly because the ship itself is always moving, churning up excesses of feeling completely inappropriate to the situation, which is, of necessity, terminally temporary. Add to that the fact that I was off on what was, for me, a great adventure.

Did you ever wonder what they did with the garbage generated by great ships like that? Not long before, I had been living near a huge garbage dump at the edge of Cambridge, Mass. I would watch the endless train of trucks coming in to dump their loads, exciting the gulls that swarmed the smouldering trash heaps like the flies of Beelzebub. At night greasy fires flared the steaming mounds of refuse with the redness of hell. And here we were in mid-Atlantic on a self-contained vessel with the population of a small city. By the end of the trip the Queen Elizabeth must have been a floating garbage dump.

Or did they throw it all overboard? Just the way the waste from the famous university town polluted its surroundings. I wonder about it now as I sit here at my computer in my comfortable apartment in Paris where I live part of each year. Up on the roof tops I can see from my window that the crow that comes over from nearby Cemetery Pere Lachaise is making uncustomary purring sounds, seductively musical, even poetic. Edgar Allen Crow.

The cemetery is where Jim Morrison is buried. His grave is the object of pilgrims from everywhere, but mostly from a sentimental mentality that makes of Dionysus an object of yearning, Dionysus, that now tired but mean, and still treacherous god. There's a story about Morrison hanging out at Max's Kansas City, the famous New York bar, when too lazy or drunk to go to the men's room, he pissed in a bottle under the table, and handed it to a starstruck waitress as a souvenir bottle of his leftover white wine. My informant always wondered whether she drank it.

The woman who arrived from the States this morning will stay over tonight at the Paris apartment. She reminds me of a girl on the Queen Elizabeth, I even remember her name because it was unusual. Nicki Nowse, rhymes with mouse, I had the impression it was an abbreviation of something

Slavic. Both of them good-natured, lavish, voluptuous, neither was to become my lover. The version on the *Elizabeth* would finally offer herself to me, and in fact I was needy. When I turned her down she couldn't understand. Actually, neither could I. "I'm not used to men refusing me," she said. I wasn't used to women offering themselves. It was an offer I couldn't refuse. And yet I did. Why? Possibly there were other considerations in my life than the Dionysian, though if so, they weren't obvious.

But why beat around the bush? Naturally I can see today, from the vantage of all the time and experience since, and by a process of triangulation making use of the various evolved intelligences with whom I now maintain contact, that at that age I was suffering from a condition of repressed spirituality that relegated my moral, esthetic and intellectual sensibilities to the unconscious. And the spiritual unconscious in a state of repression leads to a condition of spiritual perversion, in which the repressed impulses can only flare out in eruptive and often inappropriate ways.

At the time I met Federico Fellini I was still in love with a woman back in the States, though it would be more accurate to say that I was in sex, or in rut. The brute fact of sex, however, was only one factor in a relation that fulfilled repressed spiritual needs I probably didn't even know were being fulfilled, but whose satisfaction permitted release of the cruder but perhaps not more basic erotic impulses.

The very fact that I had left my lover for a year, knowing full well that the chances of picking up the relation when I returned were slim, in order to go off to Europe, shows that I must have been capable of being in love with something or things other than women at the time. Whether I knew it or not, and I didn't.

On the *Queen Elizabeth* I was in love with a blond girl, not the buxom brunette who offered herself to me but a flat chested blond girl with long straight hair who paid no attention to me. She looked very upper crust, the blond girl, so I must have been in love with the ruling class, I must have been in love with power. Also, I was in love with the way the ship's prow pared back the ocean, with the pitch and roll of a vessel on the high sea, with the rhythms of the horizon through the round port holes, I was in love with the clouds climbing over the horizon, I was in love with the changing colors of the ocean, I was in love with the adventure of voyage. And I was in love with the idea of France, where I was headed, with the high tradition of European culture. But I couldn't admit any of this was love, maybe partly because, as I know now, it wasn't what we call love. The overload we put on that word just indicates the poverty of our vocabulary. No, it was something else. But I was unable to admit even its existence.

One very surprising development for me on board the *Queen Elizabeth* was my fascination with the person I referred to as The Wife of Bath. A vigorous English lady of a certain age, as they say in France—i.e., about fifty—she was invariably on the third-class sun deck of the ship holding what might best be called court. That is, sitting up in her deck chair, gripping a mug of tea, she told stories non-stop, stories peppered with peppery commentary, often of a bawdy nature, holding in thrall a shifting audience composed however mostly, I noticed, of her countrymen. I concluded that she must be a traditional type for them, something like our cracker barrel philosopher.

The most surprising thing for me about The Wife of Bath was her sexual frankness, a quality that probably offended many Americans at the time, but which the English on board seemed to take for granted. Outspoken commentary on sexual matters, witty, vulgar, unselfconscious, was the mainstay of her discourse. Hanging out the sex laundry was not something Americans were used to in the fifties, nor do we get much of that kind of erotic ventilation now without a sense of titillation or even naughtiness. Many of her stories were explicitly pornographic, and though many of them had some point, others were obviously just for fun. But they weren't sneaky or sickoid. Her gusto was hygienic.

So The Wife of Bath suddenly opened a vision of another mode of life for me, one in which sexuality was no longer the dirty little secret that, because suppressed, became a point of reference for almost everything else. In America then sex was the repressed impulse behind power, behind morality, behind art, behind manners, behind mental illness, behind social structures, behind even and above all family life. How strange it all seemed after listening to The Wife of Bath for a while. What would Americans do without struggling with sex as evil? Would they be forced to struggle with evil as such? Have we spent so much energy on sex as evil so that we don't have to confront something else as evil? And if so, what?

In any case, next time you read Chaucer, look at "The Wife of Bath's Tale" from that point of view. It was with my lover back in Cambridge, where I'd been reading Chaucer for M.A. exams, that I first arrived at a state of total sexual satisfaction. Not that I hadn't been sexually active in my life, far from, but that was the first time I was aware of a sense of erotic fulfillment. This awareness came as if from outside of myself and not via my own reasoning powers, through the formulation that now I was ready to die. If necessary, that is. I can't explain this formulation. Why should I have been ready to die at the age of twenty-five, unless sex really has something to do with death?

It was in Cambridge that I saw Fellini's *I Vitelloni*, and there's an odd anecdote connected with that. I remember going to see it with my girlfriend feeling, as I said, contented as a well-used stud, we'd probably just gotten out of bed. But let me say something first about the life of a graduate student. Suspended as it is between the student world of the undergraduates and the professional life of professors, between the academy and the workaday quotidian, and above all, between the perfection of the written word and the abjection of the rotten world, it lacks what you might call ballast. Without friction with the ordinary contingencies and tolerating a high level of anxiety aggravated by too much work and too little pay, it tends to exaggerated swings of mood. So it's not surprising that going to see *I Vitelloni* in high spirits, I left the theater in a state of depression. Because in this story about young men trying, and failing, to break out of the banal provincial fate in which they're caught, I discovered the image of myself, and erotic accomplishments notwithstanding—which after all were in the province of any normal citizen—the prospect of my ordinary, mediocre and meaningless life.

I thought Europe was the solution. In that, I was not very different from generations of American tourists. I was especially not very different from that great wave of American tourists starting with Henry James, through Gertrude and Ezra and "Tom" Eliot, and ending with Henry Miller, the so-called exiles, though nobody was chasing them out, who collaged together a museum curator Europe that never existed, except in the minds and, more important, works of those magnificent provincials, provincials more practical and clever than their supposedly worldly hosts. If Europe doesn't work right, why not fix it? No problem. Just rearrange history a little bit, jiggle some geography, and everything comes out the way you want. Now, of course, living here, I know that their idea of Europe was the illusion of colonials who, without realizing, had outgrown their colonizers.

Except for one thing. One reality they had firmly grasped and that I too had intuited in my own uncertain way amid all the cultivated nonsense pumped into my brain by museums and foreign films and institutions of higher learning. One bit of data, slight but crucial, instantly communicated to me when I met Federico Fellini on the train to Paris.

Coming out of the theater where I saw *I Vitelloni* with my girlfriend I was, as mentioned, feeling low. It was the movie, but it was the movie probably connected with some of the other facts of my life, my seedy apartment next to the garbage dump for one, my wage slave teaching job for another, which however little time it left me for my graduate work, was better than my imminent summer job which involved eight hours of lifting heavy railroad car parts and inventorying them, starting at seven A.M. I didn't know which was worse, the boredom of the inventorying or the exhaustion of the lifting but either way, when I got back to my rubbish redolent apartment I was in no mood to hit the books for the doctorate I didn't know if I really wanted anyway. But I would nevertheless get back into it, gradually, with long minutes spent staring at the burning garbage across the street until finally, with its stink in my nose, I was able to escape into *The Faery Queen* or some such, reading long into the night with never enough sleep for the railroad yard in the morning, I knew the routine, it was a routine that would soon put me into the hospital and knock me flat on my back for a good three months. Maybe I got sick because it was the only way consciously or subconsciously I could get out of it.

In some circumstances, maybe repression of the spiritual is a means of survival. I could have handled *The Faery Queen* without the railroad yard and the garbage. I probably even could have handled *The Faery Queen* and the railroad yard, or *The Faery Queen* and the garbage. But all three at once no doubt required a depth of repression that would have reduced *The Faery Queen* to another piece of work for processing by the academic mill, or maybe simply to garbage.

Anyway, coming out of the theater with my girlfriend, and here comes the odd anecdote now, there in the middle of genteel Harvard, which I was not attending, by the way, we passed a beat-up Chevy full of the kind of tough kids I was used to from Brooklyn, but which she, as a graduate of one of the Seven Sisters out of some upper crust boarding school, obviously didn't know how to deal with. And they whistled at her. Maybe they even hooted, or made some obscene remarks, I don't remember. As I quickened my steps to get out of there, she simultaneously stopped dead on the sidewalk, turned to me, and said in a loud voice, "Hit them!" Hit them. Five or six big guys from the slums. Probably with a few clubs, baseball bats or other blunt instruments, and maybe some sharp ones as well. Oh yeah. Hit them.

But the odd thing about it, I felt at that moment as much in sympathy with them as with her. I could explain this, but do I really need to? In any case, the incident shed light. It was like being in, say, the Cinquecento in the Metropolitan Museum when all of a sudden a gigantic, muscular Mickey

Mouse walks in, looking bellicose and confused. In the U.S. today, one percent of the population owns thirty-nine percent of the wealth, and the wealth of that one percent exceeds the total wealth of the lower ninety percent of the population. The numbers probably weren't so gross at the time, but the situation is endemic. It's not a situation that's unknown, but it's not sexy. It exists as data somewhere in the national psyche, maybe out there on the garbage heap of history, everything reacts to it but it's itself inert, down the chute, it's there but not there, out of sight out of mind, we don't want to think about it, it's garbage, rotting away, dead matter, one day it will kill us too.

No doubt all of the above was a subliminal factor in my willingness to leave my girlfriend behind for Europe, in search of a better world—what a laugh—though the decision had a perverse air of desertion to it. Even for myself. In other words, I felt guilty.

At the time, I was incapable of articulating any of this, even to myself. The only thing I had enough energy to think about besides getting my work done was getting back into bed with my girlfriend. Maybe that's what sex has to do with death. Until you have enough of it—and you never have enough of it—like death, sex keeps you from thinking about anything. Especially about death. Death, the last thing you want to think about.

Not that sexuality is necessarily negative. Far from. But it can be regarded as a negative and basically is by our culture, despite the way it's merchandised. Negative maybe because sex is not something that you normally buy, and in the marketplace anything that's free is suspect. And maybe it's exactly because it's regarded as negative that it imposes on us from all sides as merchandise. I mean, what's your reaction to a no-no? Yes, yes. Right?

But Fellini. The *Elizabeth* docked at Le Havre, and then you caught the train to Paris. Which I collected my baggage and caught. I settled myself in a compartment, and then decided I was hungry, so I made my way up to the dining car, which in those days was still a linen and silver scene. It wasn't as crowded as I feared it would be, probably most people knew it was over-priced, and I was immediately seated at a table whose four places already had two occupants. I nodded at the two people opposite and stared out the window, fascinated by the differences between the intensively civilized woods and fields of France and the random wilds and acreage of the States.

My tablemates continued their conversation, they were speaking French. And they were eating a big meal, I mean it was lunch time, but this looked more like a dinner that they had ordered, or less a dinner than a repast, an empty bottle of wine on the table, a bottle of mineral water, the whole bit, as I waited for my sandwich. They were up to cheese, and they ordered another bottle of wine to go with it. He was heavy featured, disheveled but looked like he was congenitally disheveled. Though he wasn't fat, as he appears to be in photos I've seen of him since.

Meeting Fellini is an incident stored in my memory much like a photo, or rather the negative of a photo taken long ago but not developed till recently, I haven't thought about it for years. In fact, you might say that the spiritual unconscious is a take on things stored like a negative that suddenly gets developed, or develops gradually, or may never develop at all. What agency snaps that original shot I leave it to you to contemplate. Maybe it's programmed into the genetic code, or simply part of the human situation. The negative, you might even say, is the mind's denial of the world's positive, its refusal to accept things as they are. The Fellini take has developed through the intervention of Edgar Allen Crow, who visits now and then from the cemetery, as a kind of memento mori. The thought of death, I probably don't have to tell you, tends to develop a lot of negatives that otherwise remain inert in the spiritual unconscious.

Gradually it dawned on me that they were talking about American film. I started tuning in, though my French was rudimentary at the time.

" . . . Mickey Mouse," the woman said.

"And what was the name of the dog?" asked the man who I did not yet know was Fellini.

"Pluto."

"Pluto? The lord of the dead? What does that want to say?"

"It can to be that wants to say that it is as much serious as funny."

"If I remember myself well the name of the dog is Goofy. It is what?" Fellini asked.

"In Italian it is said ?potso," she said.

"Then, [?] it is to be dead to be crazy."

"How?" she asked.

"The dog."

The waiter came over to pour some wine. They stopped talking for a while to dig into the cheese. I was left to puzzle out this conversation. I found it a little mysterious. If the dog is dead to be crazy, who is the dog? And what does that mean? I could only guess he meant that death is a mad dog, which after all made some sense. In that, I mean, how do you deal with a mad dog?

I remember, even at this distance of time, that unaccountably as they were pausing for cheese and wine, my yearnings returned to the *Queen Elizabeth* and the girl with the long, straight blond hair. At some point on board I had revealed my admiration for her to a shipboard acquaintance of her social ambiance, but who was trying to escape it. He expressed surprise when I singled her out. "You mean the white death over there?" he said. On the contrary, he expressed admiration for my buxom brunette. I never asked him what he meant by the white death.

Which leads me now to wonder what would have happened had I actually hooked up with the blond and satisfied my needs for whatever I was unadmittedly craving by way of power and prestige. Because sex is never just sex, but always something else, the something else that in fact makes it sexy. Suppose I had been able to sate myself with whatever it was that I covertly desired, only to discover that wasn't what I wanted? That it was part of the garbage? My experience since suggests that would have been terminal. The white death. Mad dog country.

I was once attacked by a dog, a very large black and white dog something like a Great Dane, with jagged black splotches. It was somewhere in Spain. I was walking through some kind of wealthy neighborhood, the extremely substantial houses were mostly hidden behind whitewashed walls. I don't know why this huge dog was loose on the street, but it was, and it wasn't a stray either, it had one of those spiked collars. Out of nowhere, this dog started racing toward me with clear malign intent. Probably it felt its territory was threatened. Maybe for animals territory is the only identity. I couldn't think of anything to do other than keep walking slowly as if both unaggressive and unintimidated. The animal's head was level with the height of my shoulder. When it reached me it bared its slavering teeth and leaped in the air higher than my head, but instead of landing on me it dropped to the ground, never taking its eyes off me, and galloped on for another ten yards. Then it stopped, turned, and ran at me again, doing exactly the same thing. Strangely, it never barked, never so much as growled. It made four or five passes like that until I slowly walked out of the neighborhood. I can still recall the pattern of black splotches on its back and sides because they reminded me of a map of the British isles, the French coast and the Iberian peninsula. If I had a dog like that I would call it Europe. Or maybe my memory is playing tricks on me, maybe this is just the way, at some level, I feel about Europe. Even now I'm pitched into a state of combined defiance and anxiety when I give someone my name in Europe and they ask, "That doesn't sound American, what kind of name is that?" Reminding me that Europe still harbors much garbage that's never been sifted, much less recycled.

The network of evolved intelligences with whom I now maintain contact thinks that my meeting with Fellini had a hidden logic. In the sense that incidents materialize in the text of life only when your attention is attuned because your frame of reference makes space for them. This is what the network of evolved intelligences calls the grammar of incident, which it claims to know how to read. I might have sat next to Fellini all day and all night and never noticed him as Fellini. Or you might have. This goes for everything else, of course, from the moment you open your eyes in the morning and notice the light, which you wouldn't have noticed if you hadn't opened them. If you see what I mean. The evolved intelligences think that meeting Fellini was part of an ongoing reflex I had developed to avoid the white death. The intelligences think that for me white death avoidance had been reduced to a reflex for lack of conscious spiritual resources that probably would have made my life a lot more simple. Yes, I shoot back at the intelligences, but what do you expect from a kid still emerging from Lumpenville, U.S.A.? Mahatma Ghandi?

Edgar Allen Crow makes his presence known outside on the tiled roofs with a series of calamitous squawks that attunes my attention to a broader frame than the one my psyche reverts to if I'm not paying attention. Maybe that's his job, psyche tuning. I'm reminded of what happened next when I met Federico Fellini on the train to Paris. It was maybe then in my life that the something else not love, till then repressed, that often had moved me for unknown reasons to love things other than women, came first to my consciousness. What happened was I caught a phrase from across the table in the dining car that extracted me from my blond reverie to focus, even eavesdrop, on their conversation.

"It is a species of ?contract with the spectators, is it not? As to *La Strada* or no import what spectacle. Yes, it is very ?owl. But [?] to my advice, in the sense where life is a piece of theater, theater is ?cowly [cow-like?] a piece of life, that also."

"It is necessary not to say that to [?]. Because if life is theater why you owe for entering?"

"Name of a dog! God pork! It is there, the problem."

"For what?"

"Let us admit because [?] not museum ?decay. It is only to think about life with respect and ?antagonism. [?] I not have envy to resist with ?understanding [?]. ?Garbage [?] [?] when I made *La Strada*."

What Fellini was admitting, insofar as I could understand

what he was saying, was inadmissible to my American mentality at the time. He was admitting to the compulsive perfectionism of the spirit as against the abjection of the rotting world. He was confessing that the compulsion of the spirit was as inevitable as the garbage. The force of the to an American impractical if not intangible compulsion of the spirit is perfectly obvious when you think about it. *When* you think about it. The intelligences say that it is precisely because you don't think about it that you need to chase after the white death. Not, the intelligences will grant you, that Europeans don't chase after the white death, maybe they even chase it more, but at least they admit the helpless compulsion of the spirit as against the abjection of the rotting world.

This admission by Fellini, which I instantly if not consciously absorbed from what he said, and he didn't even say it, so I must have gathered it from the way he said what he said, was for me, according to the intelligences, one of those tiny turning points which you barely notice but which amplify and reverberate and shape the rest of your life.

I frankly don't remember what they discussed after that at the table in the dining car, but the minute I suspected that I was sitting opposite Federico Fellini, I knew I had to say something to him. Finally, as they were waiting for the change from the waiter, I blurted out in my abominable French, "Excuse me, sir, are you Federico Fellini?"

"Si?" he responded, a little defensively, I thought.

"I liked very much your film *La Strada*," I said in my abominable French.

Fellini nodded and replied in heavily accented English, "As long as the public likes it is the most important."

But I think he meant it.

Since those days, of course, Mickey Mouse has muscled into Europe in a big way. Out at Eurodisney near Paris it's still a question whether the public likes him. But Mickey is less confused now and knows what he's after. He's after Europe in the same way that Europe was once after the Americas. In the same way that the American exiles patched together their fairy tale of Europe, Mickey lays his fairy tale Europe of plastic castles over the real thing.

But what is the real thing? Maybe the real thing is no longer the actual flesh and stones of an ambiguous history but Mickey Mouse himself, now grown up and proliferating mickey mice everywhere. Maybe the real thing is what happens when the practical tom cats are away and the prodigal spirit starts to play.

starts to play   boys   massive numbers   mickey mice

boys

massive numbers

mickey mice

starts to

play   boys

mice

massive   starts

numbers boys play

mickey

starts to

boys massive mickey starts to play

mice numbers

doggy bag}########################::::::::::::::::::::--------->

A Long Narrative Poem in Prose

"Boys," said the Sybil, "you kill me."
—Petronius' *Satyricon*

1. Dracula and the Zombies

Massive numbers of American citizens have been mesmerized by subliminal messages on television, becoming Zombies programmed to act in ways beneficial to a secret sect of White Voodoo Financial Wizards.

Roland Sycamore, man of letters who under the code name Rico works secretly with the Guardian Angels Mind Liberation Unit, abruptly flies to Europe. There, his training in cultural history leads him to believe, he can find an antidote to the white voodoo mind control plague.

Paris: Bastille Day. Rico discovers that the zombie phenomenon is not limited to America. Standing among tourists from all over the world as they photograph the Arc de Triomphe, gawk at the Eiffel Tower, gape at the hotel where Hemingway lived, Rico has the eerie feeling he's dealing with the brain dead.

On this day of their national liberation the Frenchmen themselves stumble through the streets with dead eyes tossing firecrackers under the feet of pedestrians.

Place de la Bastille is jammed. There's a continuous static of firecrackers and cherry bombs. It could have been hand grenades and automatic weapons in Beirut.

Suddenly a heavyset man in a cheap green polyester suit and open shirt without collar, five o'clock shadow and bad halitosis grabs Rico by the arm:

"Pardonnez-moi, Monsieur Rico. Come wiz me."

At that moment, at a cafe table, a pasty-faced woman, vulgarly dressed, lights a firecracker, aims it carefully, and tosses it directly in Rico's path. The stranger pulls Rico forcefully to one side as the firecracker explodes in the crowd.

BLAM!

Three Japanese tourists in front of them disintegrate in chunks of flesh and spurting columns of blood.

"Whew!" says Rico. "That was no firecracker. Ugh!"

The pasty-faced woman and a Caribbean-looking Black man jump up from the table. As they disappear into the crowd, the woman looks over her shoulder at Rico and laughs, exposing a glistening row of snaggled white teeth.

That was meant for me, thinks Rico, as klaxons begin to sound.

Rico looks into the eyes of the Frenchman at his side. The two easiest ways to recognize Zombies are to look at their eyes and examine their tracks. Zombie eyes have a dead look, they look at you but they don't see you. And Zombies, odorless themselves, leave a subtle track of slime behind them that cannot so much be seen, or even felt as, after it ripens, it can be smelled.

But for those not trained in zombie lore maybe the best thing is simply to check out a sort of spiritual vacuum in the suspected Zombie, a lack of human reaction, as if others were merely wooden pieces in a big game of chess. Or Monopoly.

In fact Zombies aren't really there. They look as if they're there, but they exist only as what you might call moral holograms, a sort of ongoing absence.

Rico's companion, though, radiates a heavy sense of presence. Some combination of garlic, blood and musty earth, not quite masked by a sickeningly sweet odor of cheap cologne. But his imposing presence is more than B.O. There's something else, on a more subtle olfactory wavelength . . .

Rico has taken the standard Guardian Angel nasal training routine, side by side with the German Shepherds taught to sniff out gunmetal and explosives. Now he flips back through his mental files . . .

Of course! The Frog next to him emanates the grubby scent of someone who thinks too much, actually a typical European syndrome he's been warned about back home.

But Rico is no hick off the farm. He's been chosen for this assignment precisely because of his culture cool. Rico swings with relativism. Different tokes for different blokes.

The heavy dude leads Rico to a safe house, a seedy hotel in a distant arrondissement, and gives him a rendezvous next day at a museum. He never tells Rico his name. Maybe he doesn't have one.

The hotel turns out to be where the local whores take their clients for quickies. The pissoir is down the hall. The shitter is down the hall and down the stairs. The shower is down the stairs and across the court. The bed bugs are under the mattress. You get the idea.

Rico is in the museum standing in front of the examination of grey called *Whistler's Mother*, when a character in a soft grey fedora and dark grey cashmere cloak taps him softly on the shoulder with a cane and beckons. Rico follows him at a distance out into the damp streets.

There's something oddly familiar about this fellow, and instantly Rico realizes what it is. He's a dead ringer for Henry Kissinger. Talk about heavy.

The Paris sky is overcast. A fine drizzle fills the misty air, sifting a pearly light on greying buildings, darkening sidewalks, dappling cobbles. Wet plate glass reflects glistening asphalt.

Gradations of grey impose their subtleties on the city half-revealed in its chiaroscuro of smog-smudged limestone and green-grey copper.

Yellow-grey tree trunks punctuate the boulevards, their bare branches dripping droplets in somber puddles.

Grey-black ironwork modulates blue-grey slate and grey-white concrete.

The city is a composite of grey on grey, with grey the darker ground for fluctuating figures of grey.

This is a picture the aggressive lens of a camera couldn't make out. This is not a scene some dead-eye dick can dig. The grey rainbow is beyond the zombie spectrum, the grey rainbow of thought.

They end up in a deserted cafe in some nondescript bourgeois neighborhood and they settle at a table in a corner without a word. The man in grey looks up at Rico.

"Our original Count Dracula," he says in a deep, measured Transylvanian accent, "was a national hero for saving his homeland from the alien invader. Thus your request does not surprise me."

"Impaled them on stakes, I believe."

"Steaks? Yes. *Saignants* you might say." The obscure translinguistic pun provokes him to throw his head back in a fit of deep-throated laughter that resembles a seizure. Its effect is the more startling for the fact that he keeps his lips tight over his teeth, producing a horrible death's head effect. The laughter stops abruptly. "But in your case the stakes are equally high?"

"The stakes are America," says Rico simply. If grandly. "And the world."

"Europe has the culture you need. It was brought here with yoghurt long ago and like yoghurt has been carefully cultivated over the centuries. I can provide a starter. In Transylvania we call it Thot. It produces bacterial antibodies to voodoo brain death. The antibodies are now available in easy to take anti-stupor tabs, capsules, caplets, nasal sprays, suppositories or can be administered sonically on the airwaves as a harmless sound mix with any heavy beat punk or rock music or hidden in film and video soundtracks."

"How does it work?"

"Voodoo mind control stupifies the brain by exaggerating the dominance of the body, a phenomenon that sometimes occurs spontaneously in what you call jocks. Our culture drains the vital juices from the body so the mind can take over again."

"And what precisely do you mean by 'vital juices'?"

"In a word? Blood." He throws his head back, once again in the grip of the Ghoulish Laugh. Then just as abruptly stops and apologizes, as if he had suddenly belched.

"Your nose," observes the Kissinger look-alike, "is twitching like a rabbit's."

In fact, Rico had once again picked up that familiar grubby scent, musty, dusty, rusty, hovering around the man in grey like an almost visible shroud.

The grey man furrows his brow, his eyes go abstract then refocus. "Ah!" he exclaims. "The embarrassment of an American scenting the odor of thought. If it is not a question of data you don't know what to do with it."

"We have vitality on our side," says Rico.

"Yes. So do germs. No, the energy of the frontier counts for nothing now. The only frontier is within. Your stubborn denial of introspection is why you Americans have no immunity to the white voodoo zombie plague. You tolerate Zombies because you are all practically Zombies to start with."

The waitress puts their espressos on the table. Rico lifts his cup to his lips.

"DON'T drink that," says the grey man.

"What do you mean?"

"We didn't order coffee, did we?"

Rico looks around him. He suddenly recognizes the waitress's jagged, glistening teeth. The Caribbean-looking Black man is behind the bar. The cafe is named the Port-au-Prince.

"These are agents of Papa Doc," says the grey man. "Why not think?"

Later, back at the safehouse hotel, Rico carefully hides his precious plastic container of Thot starter in his luggage and goes to bed. But he can't sleep. He keeps thinking he hears the door knob of the room turning slowly, creaking footsteps in the hall.

Cautiously, Rico investigates his closet-like chamber, opens the door a crack to peer down the dark hall. Nobody.

Rico goes down the hall to the WC, illuminating the minuterie as he goes. But when he opens the WC the minuterie goes off, a hand reaches out the door and pulls him in by the neck and simultaneously there's a muffled thud, a grunt and a putrid odor.

When the light goes on he sees the man in the green suit with halitosis holding the limp body of the Caribbean-looking Black from the Place de la Bastille by the collar.

"Why, that's . . . !"

"Oui," says the man in the green suit, his halitosis staggering Rico. "Tonton Macoute. 'E was after zee startair." Whereupon he lifts the inert body of the Black so that his neck is exposed, and bites into the area beneath the Adam's apple.

"My god," whispers Rico.

But his protector immediately withdraws his mouth and spits, hurling the body of the Black to the floor. "Pfah!" he exclaims.

"What's the matter?" asks Rico.

"'E's emptee," responds the man in the green suit.

2. Zombie Immune Tolerance Syndrome

The 747 banks once, giving them a view of the Seine's arabesque through Paris, then wings westward.

"I have never been there," says the Kissinger look-alike, who now calls himself Mr. Grey. "Tell me what to expect in the States." He smiles lips over teeth, his peculiar death's-head smile that frankly gives Rico the creeps.

"The States are in a state of flux," responds Rico. "The different states that comprise the States are no longer united. The state of greed struggles with the state of fear. The state of confidence is undermined by the state of anguish. The state of innocence is belied by the state of ignorance."

"This is a situation highly suited for the beneficial effects of Thot," says Mr. Grey.

"What exactly does Thot mean?" asks Rico.

"The word is actually derived from the name of the ancient Egyptian god, Thoth. Thoth the Ibis-headed, Thoth the baboon. That is why the baboon is considered very intelligent in legend, whether it is or not. And that is why Mandrake the Magician carries an ibis stick. Thoth is the god of hieroglyphs and scribes, of all things written, and hence of wisdom and healing, of imagination and the moon."

"Good," says Rico. "It's known that Zombies are allergic to the moon. The moon makes them itch and squirm. They call it boredom, but exposing a Zombie to the moon is like exposing wax to heat. This is something the White Voodoo Financial Wizards can't deal with. It liberates the sense of possibility, of hope, and destroys their spell."

Rico goes back to the notebook he had been writing in. He isn't really writing, he's just eager to end the conversation. Every time Grey opens his mouth Rico gets a whiff of halitosis that spins his mind. It's not as heavy as the bad breath of the man in the green suit, but it's more penetrating. He keeps wondering what Grey's been eating.

Rico turns through the pages of the story he's writing in the notebook. Rico's cover is as a novelist, but everything he writes is really in the service of the intelligence. Everything he writes is an intelligence report. This one is called "Doggy Bag." Nevertheless, he has severe doubts about the usefulness of the intelligence in the case he's working on.

Rico knows that the Vampire tradition is aristocratic and elitist. As a result, Vampires overestimate the effect of intelligence and culture. Rico thinks the snobbist vampire myth of cultivation is mainly nostalgia for European superiority. He sees as many Zombies along the Champs-Elysee as he does on Forty-Second Street. Besides he fails to see how Europeans can make any claim about the virtues of culture and intelligence since the Holocaust.

Actually, in describing the zombie phenomenon as a voodoo conspiracy, Rico is only revealing half the truth. He doesn't want to be too discouraging. The vampire myth may be just one of the leftovers of European culture, but who knows, there may be something there. His superiors are currently grasping at straws. They want to see what Mr. Grey comes up with. Rico himself harbors high hopes for the Thot culture now stowed safely in his carry-on bag. He's always liked yoghurt.

In fact, though Zombies are being used by the White Financial Wizards for their own ends, there's a little Zombie in all Americans. What's frightening is the way that tendency is being cultivated and promoted by white voodoo with the help of the puppet-colonial forces of Papa Doc and the Tonton Macoute. Actually, what began as a conspiracy for the profit of rich corporate moguls has run totally out of control.

It used to be that Americans could tolerate their zomboid tendency but recently it seems they are completely vulnerable. The zomboid has become an unstoppable mind control plague. This vulnerability is now officially called Zombie Immune Tolerance Syndrome, or ZITS. Some even say that it was initially spread to the U.S. by Papa Doc just before his real or reputed death, a suspicion leading intelligence forces to wonder who the hell is running things around here.

Reliable reports indicate Papa Doc has himself become a Zombie to perpetuate his influence in ways we don't understand. The point is, white voodoo can be handled quietly through the old boy network, but Black voodoo is something else. Black is nether. Beyond the white voodoo intelligence. And you know what that means. It means relentless colonial pigeons may be coming home to roost.

Rico excuses himself and goes down the aisle to the toilet. Closing the door, he gets out his powerful miniaturized transmitter and his Captain Midnight Secret Service badge.

"Sycamore to Doggy Bag, Sycamore to Doggy Bag. We are bringing home the leftovers. Message follows." Rico then codes a message on his Captain Midnight badge and sends it through the transmitter. Its gist is, Baby, we may be fucked.

Thus the inauspicious beginning of Operation Doggy Bag.

3. The Get Set

The Get Set is a highly secret subversive zombie cell moving in the highest levels of white voodoo financial wizardry. The White Voodoo Financial Wizards (WVFW in these circles,) having created the Zombie to do their bidding at lower levels of society, simply cannot see that they are themselves infiltrated by their frankensteinian creations. This blindness sometimes reaches an extreme at which a Wizard himself has become a Zombie without realizing it.

Probably the most eminent specimen of this sort was Richard Nixon, a crypto-zombie known in the trade as Dead

Eye Dick. What else could account for his blindness and the ensuing scandals? Insiders say William Casey was a Zombie dupe, and that his behavior toward the end of his life was no coincidence. The CIA Director dies on cue, taken fatally ill the day he's to testify? I ask you.

Oh yes, every now and then there are purges that hit the headlines, but the process of infiltration goes on. Once the Zombie Syndrome has been created there's no way of stopping it. ZITS has its way of infecting everyone's personality. No one is immune, because the White Voodoo Financial Wizards have with great care and persistence through the years eroded our zombie immune systems for their own ends. We are all now to a greater or lesser degree victims of ZITS. Including the Wizards themselves.

So the revolt of the Zombies becomes more and more inevitable.

Rico and Mr. Grey get out of a taxi in front of a pricey New York bistro in Lower Manhattan called the Odeon. Elegant Yuppy stockbrokers and casually chic citizens of the Hipoisie stream in and out of the posh bohemian bar and restaurant, picking their svelte way among bag ladies combing through trash cans and street people with rag-laden supermarket carts, suave dolls and dudes in swellagant duds dodging panhandlers as blithely as they maneuver through the pâté crazed mob at Balducci's.

It's party time in Tribeca. The festive crowd in the Odeon spills out onto the streets. A fox trot hangs in the air, and several pallid couples, the women with mouths gaping in romantic self-indulgence, the men with eyes narrowed in macho intent, dance gaily across the sidewalk and over the curb, carelessly grazing the veering fenders of long limousines as they pull in and out, boarding and discharging opulent passengers. But something about the lighthearted funseekers, perhaps the way they move a bit too formally, or the way they seem to disappear when they turn sideways, strongly suggests that hologrammatic quality peculiar to Zombies.

Rico and Mr. Grey are accompanied by Z, their Guardian Angel. Supposedly assigned to Rico and Grey as security, Z is actually a zombie mole whose cover is so effective that his true identity is unknown even to himself. Z is an international man-about-town, currently trying to work his way into the Get Set. Z is fascinated with the slice of high life on display here. He stares intensely at these sophisticated men and women, he stares almost, it seems to him, through them. New to New York, Zombies are news to him. He doesn't know what these people are, never having seen a Zombie before. Or so he thinks. Zombies don't recognize one another as Zombies, that's one of the signs of being a Zombie. So if you've never seen a Zombie now you know why.

The trio of observers do not, however, join the happy throng of merrymakers. Instead they find their way to the office of the restaurant where they have a business appointment. They are engaged in a campaign to insinuate Thot into the United States, and what better way than to hook the influential Get Set, role models for consumers everywhere. Besides, in its relentless quest for new things to get, the Get Set is always ready to go with anything novel. Thus the common saying, "ready, Get Set, go."

In this case the novelty, concocted by Guardian Angel counter-marketing experts, is a product called Cold Thot, a frozen slush desert with fewer calories than ice cream and a more provocative texture than frozen yoghurt. ("In France taste is called goo. In America Cold Thot is all goo.") The product is catching on and the Thot culture is spreading. Rico is optimistic because he knows that Thot is the active ingredient in culture and intelligence. But he also knows that products developed on the basis of European research sometimes don't travel well across the Atlantic, and when a European culture like Cold Thot mixes with American bacteria the result could be tepid mush. Thot turned to goo in ad copy does not augur well, but Rico has got to figure that Thot in any form is better than no Thot at all.

When they're done in the office they move on to the bistro itself where they meet some of the luminaries of the Get Set. Stylish Phil "Fruit Fly" Flush, who made a fortune cornering the kiwi market is there with gaunt but lush-lipped young British fashion model, Velva "Sucky" Tosh. Tory-toned talking head Bill Buck, noted for a complexion of one who eats garbage, is talking up his new organization, Tribecans for the Trilateral Commission.

But most exciting of all, our trio gets to meet the uncrowned king of the Get Set, young Spar Getty, with his wife Betty. Spar Getty is a well known sportsman, an enthusiast of yacht racing and boxing, and is notorious for his love of Italian cuisine. Both Spar and Betty are into collectibles, and Betty buys not only art but art galleries, art movements and museums.

Mr. Grey is a little overwhelmed by the volume of white noise in the establishment. He feels as if he's walked into a carnival. But he has, of course, read the Russian critic Bakhtin, and understands that the carnival is a key to secular culture in its inversion of all that is sacred. Mr. Grey is always delighted to stand the sacred on its head. He is a follower of the Great Beast of the Apocalypse and believes degeneration must precede regeneration. At least decadence is a recognition of the sacred however diabolical, and sorts well with his own tendencies. While a Zombie just looks at you with dull incomprehension when you speak about the sinful joys of wanton sacrilege. Zombies are such populists.

Spar Getty comes over to have a word with Mr. Grey. "We are aware of your efforts to cultivate Thot in our country," he says. "And let me assure you we will do anything we can to help. We want your input on establishing a Thot institute to put Thot on a firm foundation. We need a well-sanitized Thot Tank. Thot is already fermenting here and we are concerned that it be kept pure. Just give us some numbers."

Mr. Grey is charmed. Though aware that this may be just more white noise, it occurs to him that white noise, which seems to be used here to drown out creative thought, may be complementary to the black holes he is familiar with in the old country, which are similarly used to bury everything unthinkable.

Mr. Grey will soon discover that he is mistaken. But only after it is too late.

"Insiders have reason to worry about purity these days," Spar Getty confides. "People already whisper about characters like 'Fruit Fly' Flush, about Mafia connections, about a so-called WVFW, about crypto-Zombie infiltrators and an outbreak of ZITS. Insiders are cryptic because our power comes from the crypt. We don't need drunken fermentations of Thot adding to the chaos. Not that Cryptonians dislike chaos. As long as we can control it. Cryptonians are born to control. We feel that people like you understand us. People like Kissinger, Brezinski, Teller. People with deep, masculine voices and a taste for red blood. The best of Europe, none of your peasant riff-raff, *hein*?"

Getty drifts into the crowd and Velva Tosh sidles up to Mr.

Grey, vamping him with her eyelashes. Suddenly her eyes fix on him and he can see the muscles working in the hollows of her pallid cheeks, the wings of her nose fluttering, as she struggles to articulate something. "I say . . . "

"That's right," says Mr. Grey. "It takes one to know one. How are the pickings?"

"Juicy," she replies.

"What do you see in this Fruit Fly fellow, if you don't mind my asking?"

"He's nice and fat. Good to suck. Forget the others here. They're empties."

"You mean . . . ?"

"Afraid so. The Zombies have gotten to them."

"Then, that explains this sort of cardboard quality. In a way I'm disappointed. I thought it was a manner."

"Would that they had the imagination."

"You mean . . . they're sincere?"

"Utterly. About everything they say. Even when it's hypocritical."

"Tch, tch."

"Quite. For the real thing you avoid the Get Set. The Get Set is unsettled, they're always chasing around. For the real thing you have to infiltrate Gotts Knot circles. If you prefer the real thing. I do but some don't. I find them the juiciest. It's a matter of, uh, taste. They're the heart of the WVFW. The Gotts Knots got everything tied up, and they've had it tied up for a long time. And what they haven't got they're busy getting."

"For example."

"For example? Gene farms. It's an extension of the old agribusiness. One of my Gotts Knot friends, Dr. Frank Stein, owns patents on the production of human parts. Designer body replacements. Others are aiming to colonize the planets. Everything will be reduced to a few trademarks. From the solar plexus to the solar system. By the way, a word to the wise. These people will tell you they have a real stake in Thot. But if it starts to ferment, watch out. That stake may turn up in your heart. They'll send their errand boys after you quick."

"And who might they be?"

"You know the genre. The idea doctors. The guard dogs of the mind. If nothing goes in, nothing comes out. If anything does come out call it pretentious and bury it in static."

"I see. So if white noise doesn't do the trick here they resort to the old black hole?"

"Black holes went out with Dr. Freud. Just keep your fangs clean and beware of Dr. Faust. In America he sells his soul for an invitation to the ball."

But Mr. Grey never gets it straight, the difference between America and Europe, and this makes him easy prey for Zombie idea doctors. He persists in confusing white noise with black holes, while the European talent for repression has nothing in common with the American strategem of sincerity and getting everything out on the table. It's the difference between innocence and cynicism, and any child knows that innocence, as a practice, will overwhelm cynicism every time. Unlike Europeans, Americans are innocent until proven guilty.

In practice innocence means you can entertain all sorts of ideas, even contradictory ones, as equally valid until proven otherwise, like brand names in a supermarket. You sense you don't have a stake in any of them and maybe you're right, at least any of them in the supermarket. What difference do they make in your life? This means they all cancel one another out. This means you don't have to think about anything.

This is what white noise is all about. It's all about not thinking about anything, which leaves you free to pursue your basic self-interest, what the hell, while giving yourself the satisfying impression that you're thinking about everything. White noise is the moral equivalent of Great Books or the Grand Tour of Culture from Paris to Peking.

So when Bill Buck introduces Mr. Grey to producer Rod Drackenstein, Mr. Grey thinks it's all about a movie that will help cultivate Thot. He doesn't understand that Thot is just another consumer product to Drackenstein, like shoes, or bananas. "You sell Thot, I sell entertainment. What's the difference?" Drackenstein says, a remark that Mr. Grey takes to be a declaration of common interest. Rico tries to warn him that Drackenstein is only interested in one thing, and it's the same thing that Spar Getty is interested in, which is why he's underwriting the project.

"Forget his talk about collecting collectibles," says Rico. "Never mind his efforts for America's Cup, his campaign for pasta for the poor, his grandiose disquisitions about low income housing on the planet Crypton. That's all white noise. He's after you because you're European and that means Eurodollars, and Eurodollars are international, untaxed, unregulated, unsecured, machine washable and so liquid they're almost vapor. America's Cup is filled with Eurodollars."

"I'll slip some Thot into it," says Mr. Grey. "You only need a little to ferment the whole batch."

But this only gives the thought doctors an opening which they are quick to take advantage of. Suddenly there are sinister headlines: "EUROTHOT TURNS TO GOO." "FOREIGNERS DILUTE U.S. INTELLECTUAL CAPITAL."

And so the witch hunt begins. The townspeople march on the castle, so to speak, led by zombie idea doctors and thought surgeons, the intellectual witch doctors whose banner is "credibility." Credibility means credited by those with sufficient credit in the bank to publish, promote and disseminate to the credulous what is accredited by those with the right intellectual credentials to be credible to those with the credit. The amount of credit that someone like Spar Getty commands is incredible, which is the way he prefers it. Yet even the Get Set defers to the incredible credibility of a man like I. Gott, whose credit is not to be believed and who, to give him credit, is totally indifferent as to whether you believe it or even whether you believe Gott is or Gott's not. But whether you give credence to Gott or not, you're part of his plot. The existence of Gott is so pervasive as to be beyond belief. Unbelievable or not, much of what you've done you've done for Gott, and then forgot.

In the unmentionable name of Gott, then, the errand boys of credibility lead the rabble to the castle to protect their native beliefs. The structure that poor Mr. Grey has tried to erect on the basis of Cold Thot is torched by torchlight, red on sweaty faces. Mr. Grey is impaled on a stake and left dangling, with a sign on him that says, "Pretentious." The idea doctors then rush off to the Gotts Knot ball.

When Rico arrives at the castle, Mr. Grey is still alive. He has time to mutter three words: "Sicksicksick." Then he expires, leaving Rico to wonder why Grey needed to underline the obvious with his last breath. As he is about to walk away, Rico remembers that Mr. Grey was a devotee of the Great Beast of the Apocalypse, whose occult number is six six six. Rico immediately turns back to the castle and heads for the safe in Mr. Grey's office. He dials six six six on the combination lock and, sure enough, the safe clicks open.

Inside the safe Rico finds a sheet of paper with a mysterious message scrawled on it. The message reads, "prescription: inscription." Rico immediately grasps its momentous import. Just before he was lynched by the townspeople, evidently, Mr. Grey had stumbled on the antidote to the American bacteria that kept turning Cold Thot to goo. The prescription is inscription. That is, in order to counteract the white noise of information that interacts with Cold Thot to create meltdown, obviously, you need to create a more stable form of Thot. You need a form of Thot that remains stable at room temperature and yet retains the qualities that make it a superconductive medium compared to all other media.

Thot maintains maximum stability and conductivity through inscription. In Europe, perhaps, with its force of tradition, oral transmission might do the trick, or power of example, either from person to person or through the media. But in America nothing is resistant enough to meltdown from white noise other than inscription. Writing is the lock against the flood of white noise. And reading is the key.

Rico immediately gets out his minitransmitter and his Captain Midnight Secret Service badge. "Sycamore to Doggy Bag, Sycamore to Doggy Bag. Don't eat lunch. Coming home with the leftovers." Then he encodes the following cryptic message on the Captain Midnight badge. *What the frag meant: From the feast of their cultures, the fast food of our vultures. Squawk. Yawp. Co co rico. These riffs are sure against their runes. T. S.*

4. The Revolt of the Zombies

The zombie masses are controlled through a carefully calculated ongoing TV serial which they are persuaded is the way things are in reality. When the Zombies revolt they actually try to impose this never-never land on the course of history, throwing their former masters into panic as society disintegrates in anarchic brutality.

Zombies really do believe that the point is to want it all. Why shouldn't they want it all? If they don't want it all somebody else will want it all and they believe that people who want it all get it all. If they don't want it all they won't get it all and where will that leave them? Without anything at all, they believe.

Zombies really do believe that if somebody tries to stop you from wanting it all you pull a gun and blow him away. It doesn't have to be a gun, it could be a lawyer. You could pull a lawyer and blow him away. Or you could pull a politician, if you could afford one. Or whatever. It's just that a gun is the cheapest and the handiest. So you pull whatever you can pull and if you don't like it, fuck you. It's the Fuck You Decade.

The Revolt of the Zombies is a situation in which everyone is carrying on his own private revolution in complete isolation from everyone else's private revolution. It's the privatization of revolution. It's revolutionary free enterprise. Entrepreneurs are selling revolution as a consumer item. Even the government engages in revolutionary free enterprise on the side. Governments have rights too.

None of this is explicable without Zombie revolt. The problem is nobody knows how to deal with Zombie revolt because Zombie revolt describes a situation in which the soap opera of reality has disintegrated into fragments nobody knows how to deal with. It turns out that even the Voodoo Financial Wizards have no scenario when it comes to disintegration. For them too the fabric of experience is unraveling into a tangle of random threads. The stock market plummets.

The knee jerk response of the Voodoo Financial Wizards when confronted with a problem is to package it and sell it. Among the more successful packages the voodoo market experts have thought up are PoMo and New Age, two trade marks targeted at slightly different sectors of the market. They are really the same product because they both exploit the same marketing technique, the famous "pet rock ploy" of selling nothing in the name of something. It's true, promotion is expensive, but production is cheap.

PoMo and New Age are successful marketing strategies because they are full of a haunting quality of emptiness which appeals to Zombies because they are full of the same thing. But emptiness as an ingredient makes a product highly unstable if not totally ephemeral. Maintenance is difficult. What do you with emptiness when it stops working? Resale value is nil. Investment possibilities are mysterious. When this becomes obvious it leads to aggravated fragmentation of the unraveled fragments that led to the original fragmentation. Everybody's private revolution turns ugly. The results are truly revolting.

One revolting result is an orgy of get. In the absence of a coherent soap opera as a guide, a Zombie will decide the natural thing to do is to try to get it all. But it's easy to see that if each person tries to get it all there isn't going to be enough for all to get. Another revolting result is a war of all against all. This situation fosters mistrust. Millions of private revolutions raging at the same time add a fifty-first state to America, the state of fear.

Before we ask why Zombies are revolting we have to ask why Zombies are Zombies. And the answer is fear, according to Rico. Fear is the root of vice and the root of avarice. Deep, unnameable, unrecognized, numbing fear.

"Zombies are scared shitless," says Rico. "Have you ever seen a Zombie shit? I defy anyone to show me a piece of zombie shit. You may have thought that Zombies are constipated but let me put you straight. Zombies are shitless because they've been scared shitless. What did you expect? Wouldn't you be scared shitless if you'd been plunged into a living death and then revived only for purposes of enslavement?

"Don't get me wrong, I don't put down Zombies as a class," says Rico, "I'm not a racist, even where Zombies are concerned. I especially like Zombie girls, a Zombie girl will fuck anything and I like girls who will fuck anything, especially if it's me. But Zombie girls prefer Zombie boys because Zombie boys don't require any reaction or above all sentience. And because Zombie boys, scared stiff, go around with permanent erections, even after they come they have erections, they don't even know they have erections. Did you ever know a Zombie boy who was even rumored to have a fit of impotence? Of course not. A Zombie boy hasn't got the brains to be impotent if his life depends on it, that is, not the operational brains, the consciousness, who gives a fuck about inert brain matter anyway, it might just as well be mashed potatoes. A Zombie boy could fuck a shark without being impotent, what does he know? Zombies always have a hard-on for something, I mean it doesn't even matter what it is, it's just a question of more more more, it could be earth worms, or old pickle jars, or real estate, or tax exempt municipal bonds, or used scum bags."

Well you get the idea. Zombies, however brainy, are dumb. Because numb is dumb. But when the ice suddenly breaks, look out.

The mass murders start in California and then spread to Texas. Soon there are outbreaks all over the States. Some Zombie suddenly mumbles *I've had it*, picks up whatever weapon happens to be at hand, and starts slashing, clubbing or shooting whoever happens to be around. When he runs out of steam he turns on himself, if he has any energy left. People start making bets on the number of the next set of victims. A Guinness Book of Records category is established. The National Rifle Association conducts a crash campaign to legalize Uzi machine guns and grenade launchers so that innocent citizens can protect themselves. The TV networks increase the number of police shows in prime time, displacing national news for programming that both reassures viewers that the authorities are in control and satisfies the growing public taste for violence.

It is, however, an apparently minor sidelight of the spreading mass murder epidemic that Rico finds of interest for his investigation. In a number of instances, newspaper accounts mention the presence of a strange figure at or near the site of a mass murder. This figure appears only at night and on the occasion of a full moon. Hirsute and fanged, the most striking thing about this apparition is its singing. It sings to the moon, wordless songs, moans and howls and gutturals and grunts, changeable as the song of a mockingbird, songs that have a strange effect on any Zombie that happens to hear them, songs that make Zombies weep. This figure, quickly assumed in the popular mind to be responsible for the mass murders, is dubbed by journalists the Wolfman.

Rico is not so sure that the Wolfman deserves the mass murder rap. It doesn't figure. On every occasion on which the Wolfman is reported to be present at a mass murder, a perpetrator is also found weeping in a state of despair and repentance. And on every occasion the Wolfman is present and a perpetrator is not found, there is no mass murder, but there is invariably a weeping Zombie. This leads Rico to conclude that, far from being responsible for the mass murders, the Wolfman in some way is able to abort them, probably by making the potential Zombie perpetrators weep. Rico realizes that if he can discover how the Wolfman aborts mass murders by making Zombies weep, he will be able to end the mass murder epidemic, and perhaps the ZITS plague as well.

There follows a race between Rico and the blood hounds of law enforcement to track down the Wolfman. Rico quickly discovers that the Wolfman likes to stop at zoos to get the news. After many weeks of zoo hopping, Rico finally picks up the trail just ahead of the posse in the mountains of Colorado, in a wolf preserve at a place called the Inn of the Black Wolf. He tracks the Wolfman through Wolf Creek Pass where he loses the trail, then picks it up again at Wolftrap. By this time the mass murders have evolved into serial mass murders. In Colorado there's been a series of mass murders by a Zombie known only as "the Lump Gulch killer," because Lump Gulch is thought to be where he lives. The track of the Wolfman leads Rico up a forgotten mountain path to an abandoned rail line through unused Needle's Eye Tunnel to the east side of the continental divide, where he soon finds himself in the isolated venue of Lump Gulch.

Up in Lump Gulch tonight the wind is calm, the moon is full. The snow glitters on the peaks. Rico at first thinks the howling is the wind, then remembers that there is no wind. The howling gets louder and louder as he works his way through the pines. Suddenly, he comes upon a bizarre scene in a clearing. A weeping Zombie sits on a fallen log, his shotgun next to him on the ground, while his cowering family looks up at a high rock with a collective expression of awe. Rico follows their gaze, and there on the rock is the Wolfman, singing away at the moon.

Approaching the rock carefully, Rico tries to make his presence known to the lupine figure. At first it takes no notice. "Arr-OOOOOO," it bays. "Arr-OOOOOO." When it sees Rico crawling up the rock it bares its fangs and snarls. But Rico, intuiting that the snarl is more defensive than aggressive, continues to approach, trying at the same time to indicate his peaceful intentions via sign language. "Grrr," says the Wolfman. "Growf."

"Arrooof, arrooof," says Rico all of a sudden. He doesn't know how it came to him to say that. But he says it again. "Arrooof, arrooof." The Wolfman, hearing a language he understands, gets down on all fours. Rico, too, suddenly finds himself on all fours. He scampers up to the Wolfman and sniffs him from the front, then he sniffs him from the back. Through the rank animal smell Rico perceives another smell, a smell of something like warm wool, a smell which, as soon as he smells it, gives him the urge to weep. If the rank smell is a smell of pure ferocity, the woolly smell is the smell of pure kindness.

Rico lies down on his stomach and lets the tears come. Great sobs well up from his belly. He forgets to think about anything. He lies there listening to the Wolfman, whose song has resumed now, listens to him baying at the moon, listens to his howls and moans and growls and rhythmic grunts, he sounds a lot like James Brown at times, and in his more meditative phases something like Billie Holiday. At times Rico thinks he can almost make out words, almost but not quite. The song comes to the edge of words, plays around with wordness, but never quite crosses the boundary from music to words. It's like listening to a completely strange foreign language that can't be deciphered without a translator. It comes to Rico that he is going to be the translator. It will be left to him to write down the words so that others can look at the words and recapture the song.

Abruptly Rico hears a final grunt and the Wolfman crumples, collapses bleeding into Rico's arms. Immediately Rico knows what's happened. The posse, with its high-powered, infra-red, heat-seeking telescopic rifles, is now within range, and someone got in a lucky shot. Rico can tell that the Wolfman is a goner, but he's still conscious. The Wolfman indicates that he wants to talk, and he starts talking in a human voice. As he talks, Rico realizes that he looks familiar and then—could it be?—yes, the Wolfman is actually his old zombie mole double agent Guardian Angel security guard, Z.

Rico knows, from the nature of the terrain he's just crossed, that they have at least a half an hour before the posse arrives. He listens carefully as Z tells him the story of how he became a part-time animal, with powerful animal powers, and above all the power, by making people feel more like animals, to make them feel more like people.

By the time the Wolfman is done talking, Rico knows many things. But one thing he knows for sure: if he ever had to do it all over again, he'd do it with animals.

Taking his last breath, Z presses Rico's hand, murmuring. "It's up to you now," Z says. "Write it down." Then he goes limp.

5. The Story of Z

There exists in Italy a concept known as mano morto, "dead hand," through which, for example, you can allow your hand to molest a sex object of your choice in a bus or other crowded public place without knowing anything about it yourself. This concept was brought to the Caribbean by Columbus, where it later merged with Voodoo doctrine to produce the typical corpo morto of the zombie ritual. When the new Zombie arises from corpo morto he is in a permanent state of cranio morto, or "dead head." This is simply an extension of the concept of mano morto to the entire being. Thus, for example, a Zombie can actually fuck somebody without knowing anything about it, or he can fuck somebody up without knowing anything about it. I have even known Zombies to totally fuck themselves up without knowing anything about it. Zombies have perfected the zipless fuckup.

The *cranio morto* of a Zombie is impenetrable. Anytime a Zombie is threatened with consciousness he races out and buys something, it doesn't matter what. "When the going gets tough, the tough go shopping," as they say. Under these circumstances the Zombie will go into a frenzy of get. Get get get. Also he jogs. Many Zombies jog. Not all joggers are Zombies by any means, the Zombies are the ones who jog with the muzak plugged into their ears.

The *mano morto* of the soul that afflicts Z occurred through an initial and continually reverberating shock of fear. Z is not exactly sure what happened. He was very little. Some big people came, he seems to remember uniforms, and shut him up in a dark, smelly, suffocating place. He thinks it might have been a car trunk or box car because it moved. He remembers worrying about how he was going to get food. He remembers screaming. He remembers an odor of gas. He remembers the odor of burning flesh. He remembers falling and being told, *Go to sleep, go to sleep*. Finally he did but he wasn't asleep he was dead.

When he woke up he knew they had done something to him and everything was different. He knew they had done something to him and nobody would tell him what. The next thing he remembers is going to school and being told to behave or else they'd do it to him again and this time it would be worse. From then on everything he did was based on or else. Do this or else. Do that or else. And by god he did it. He did it faster and he did it better than anybody. And above all he did it more. Or else.

You can now understand why Z eventually becomes a member of the Get Set. His zomboid character, rather than conflicting with his meteoric rise into the highest circles of white voodoo financial wizardry, actually adds propulsive energy. First of all Z, like all Zombies, has no idea he's a Zombie. When he's recruited as a zombie agent he thinks he's being recognized for his basic superiority rather than being identified as one who does things only or else. But then, who knows these days who is a Zombie and who isn't? The Shadow knows, but he's not telling. The Shadow reports only to Papa Doc.

Z's ability to hone his personality into an acute state of pure, blind financial agency makes him a perfect spy in the Get Set. The more so in that he doesn't know he's a spy. Nor does he understand that most of the other members of the Get Set are Zombies. He fits right in. He's a natural good boy. He just does what everybody naturally wants done and says what everybody just naturally wants to hear and everybody likes him. It's a natural formula for success. After a trial period of being a natural good boy he becomes a natural good old boy. At the very first vacancy he naturally wins a nomination to the old boy network. Some might be satisfied with this, but his Zombie nature demands more, more, more. It's the zombie curse never to be satisfied with what you have and to feel sorry for yourself over what you don't.

Persecution reversal is a sure sign of zombiehood. The Knotsies, predecessors of the Gotts Knot, were the first Zombies in the modern sense. Caught up in a mass murder scam, they were always whining about the difficulties involved in dispatching their victims. This is typical. A Zombie Nobel Prize winner, for example, will genuinely feel oppressed, deprived and persecuted, and will be driven to yet more desperate prodigies of zombie effort to improve his lot. A Zombie President, like Dead Eye Dick, will feel spat upon and therefore will harbor royal ambitions, while the succeeding occupants of the White House, as gippers gipping the nation with white noise, felt no need to be anything other than the atavistic Vampires that they were.

It's the zombie curse always, at all times, to feel like a failure at bottom. Because Zombies do things not simply to do things but to do things or else.

It's during his Get Set phase that Z meets lush-lipped Velva "Sucky" Tosh and is mugged by love. Zombies can't exactly fall in love, but they experience something like it as a mysterious assault on one's autonomy, just as they feel sex as an invasion of one's anatomy. Z, of course, has no idea that Velva is a Vampire. Zombies, knowing nothing about themselves, know even less about others beyond the fact that they are objects of merchandising. Therefore Z is untroubled by the insurmountable problems that arise in the pairing of a Zombie and a Vampire. Basically, Vampires want blood and Zombies don't have any, while Zombies crave consumption and Vampires are unconsumable, immortal. Z has a friendly merger in mind but the bottom line is that Vampires can't merge, they can only acquire.

Vampires have one big advantage, however. They are immune to ZITS. But Zombies are not immune to The Mummy's Curse, the curse of the living dead. The kiss of the Vampire is basically a way of spreading the curse of the living dead. As victims of *cranio morto*, Zombies are already living dead. So they don't worry about infection from that dread disease unleashed on the western world when it violated the pharaohs' tombs in the course of its colonial rape of the third world. The intentional numbness required for that violation was punished by The Mummy with a disease that strikes its victims not only numb but dumb. Just as the initial terrifying rout of the third world by Count Dracula in Medieval Rumania returns amplified in the Vampires' reign of terror.

Zombies, themselves native spawn of the third world, don't worry about The Mummy's Curse. They are too numb to worry. They are the third world's numb response to an even greater and more oppressive numbness. Yet they say that even Baby Doc suffers from The Mummy's Curse.

So numbness becomes a virtue for Z as, in certain conditions, stupidity can be an advantage. Who else but a Zombie would be dumb enough to fuck a Vampire? Yet from the mutual ecstasy of a Vampire and a Zombie strange events will flow.

Insects. Insects are the spawn when Z and Velva mate. Albino insects. The moment Z withdraws they start to swarm out of her vagina, buzzing, clicking, chirping, not just one kind of insect but a whole handbook of insects, hopping, crawling, flying out in a glistening white conga line of insects. The collective sound they make is repulsively familiar to Z. "Zzzzzz," they go. "Zzzzzz zzzzzz zzzzzz."

"My god," he says to Velva. "It's . . . white noise!"

When Velva verifies the truth of this observation, horrified, and before Z can do anything about it, she moves to end her own life. She employs the standard method, and the only one available to despairing Vampires since, as we know, Vampires have a reputation for being immortal. Velva whips out a garlic-coated silver dagger with a handle shaped like a cross, and plunges it into her heart.

"Velva!" exclaims Z. "Why . . . ? What . . . ?"

"It's . . . Mummy's Curse," gasps Velva. "The living dead . . . can only reproduce . . . through insects. It's the white . . . " Velva loses consciousness.

Z lifts her by the shoulders and shakes her. ""Velva! Sucky!"

She opens her eyes. " . . . noise that . . . spawns . . . numb . . . mumm . . . " Her eyes fall shut. She collapses all bloody into his arms.

As Velva relaxes into death, her face undergoes a strange transformation. Its voluptuous look of carnal and decadent sensuality is gradually replaced by an expression of innocent sweetness and purity. Z is startled, then repelled. He flings her lifeless body from him. This is not the candid, mature succulence he loves, but some horrid little girl piece of hypocrisy. Snow White. It's the White Death. The White Death is the spiritual equivalent of white noise.

Z doesn't understand what's happened, what he feels. He feels he needs more information. At least he feels something. Feeling is more information.

Data. Data in the static of white noise. Hard fact will save him. Z couldn't be further from the truth. Without realizing it, Z has been infected with The Mummy's Curse by Velva. Even Zombies can catch The Mummy's Curse from insects if they don't use insecticides during intercourse. He is now not only a victim of *cranio morto* but also of rigid digit, the curse of the living dead. People with rigid digit are so numb they can express their numbness only through numbers, not only numb but mum—bitter fruit of The Mummy's Curse. It is typical of those afflicted with rigid digit to imagine that information can save them. It is the rigid digit bunch who invented the digital computer. Problem is, they have the hardware, but they don't have the software.

People with hardware imagine information can save them but they are imagining things. Imagination is funny. Imagination draws on information but deletes the nits and grits that don't fit into the program. That's because the brain is a white noise machine. But every now and then you have to expose yourself to the gritty knit of experience. Leave nothing to the imagination. The imagination is a dead tooth, dead at its root in experience. The imagination is an abscess that threatens to leave us nerve dead, life numb.

The brain may be a white noise machine but it also has a compulsion to discern patterns in things, even in white noise. Even in snow on a television screen. If there is no figure then the ground becomes the figure. If things don't figure then we look to the ground. And the ground is what we all have to stand on.

The most interesting things are the things left over after you notice the things you notice. The things you don't notice, that is, the things you forget not after but as you see them, are the things that make no kind of sense. Or they make another kind of sense, a sense that you don't, can't, or don't want to see. Raw data. The leftovers of reality. Double data, because you both see it and don't see it. What Z comes to call the datta.

Z has a problem with The Mummy's Curse. It is only the datta that can save us from the Mummy, Z feels. Z is wrong, but on the right track. Feeling is part of the software. Your imagination has become part of the hardware. Your imagination is pre-recorded. Your imagination is installed by the White Voodoo Financial Wizards. When you begin to see beyond it to the datta, you begin to establish a datta base. But information is not knowledge. To express the datta base as knowledge you need to process it with the software.

Z tries to get back into the swing of Get Set life, but he's not in the swing of things anymore. That is, he's not swinging with some things but he's beginning to swing with other things, though he doesn't realize this yet. Z isn't as getty as he used to be, he doesn't have that permanent hard-on for get. Part of him wants to forget all that. He goes through all the motions for getting something forgetting he doesn't have a hard-on for getting it. The result is he doesn't get it.

Z decides to retire from life for a while. He thinks that if he thinks about it for a while he might get it. Despite the atavistic Vampires in the White House at the time, and the worldly tone of get they set, he thinks it's time to withdraw and defocus.

Defocussing is a medical procedure invented by ophthalmologists to relax the eyeballs. In order to defocus you go into a room dark enough to stop you from seeing the things you usually see and stare at a blank wall long enough to start seeing things you couldn't see before. The initial reaction to this process is almost always impatience, followed by dread. But better dread than dead. Dread is part of the software.

Z has to go through the stage known as unlocking the dread lock. Once the dread lock is unlocked it's not so much dreadful as it is a shock. Z becomes aware of the white noise of his brain, the snow in his retina, the static in his ear. This stage is known as getting to know the medium. The medium is part of the software. When you get to know the medium you realize that the medium is yourself.

As a medium Z becomes the medium for a lot of datta but the result is that he's overwhelmed. He doesn't know what to do with all that datta. That's because he's still a victim of The Mummy's Curse. When he tries to express all that datta all he can do is stay mum.

Z stumbles out into the street in a state of confusion. In his defocussed condition all the datta coming in at him makes him blink and sneeze. An overflowing wire trash basket imposes a disconcerting volcano of discomposition, disrupting his field of vision. Scraps and leftovers of the ship of state boil out of the basket, soiled newspapers, green and red soda cans, bits of sandwich, an old men's shoe of indeterminate color, crumpled tan paper bags, a blackened banana peel. Datta.

An ambiguously-aged bag person, dressed in ragged layers and rolling a shopping cart whose contents are bundled in sacking and plastic. The bag person approaches the trash basket and starts sorting through. It picks a sandwich bit from the basket, examines it in the hand, holds it up to regard, stuffs it into the mouth. Datta.

Miscellaneous spare parts of the commonwealth drift through the streets, apparently invisible to Zombies on their daily rounds, huddle in doorways in twos and threes, collect on street corners, gather in subway stations sleeping on benches or brooding in silent knots, doing nothing, sometimes sullen, sometimes shouting to one another, sometimes washing your windows at intersections, menacing in some vague way. Z has always seen them and has always immediately forgotten them, as if they weren't there, until he sees them the next time. Datta.

Z is surprised, even embarrassed, to realize he has a huge erection. He'd thought he was done with all that, but then he understands why this erection is different from erections of the past. It's that this erection is not a hard-on for anything. It comes to him like a gift, an inspiration, spontaneous and beyond control. And he understands that he is not in control, neither in his own control nor anyone else's. This is how datta turns into yatta.

You're in the stage of yatta when you realize your mojo is working. Your mojo is part of the software. You realize your mojo is working when you feel it's not rigid anymore, when you know it's swinging. It's a hard feeling to describe and it's a soft feeling to describe but you know it when you feel it. Sometimes you're up, sometimes you're down. Sometimes you're smiling, sometimes you frown. Sometimes you're happy, sometimes you're sad. But when you're unhappy, it ain't all that bad. Sometimes you're soft when you'd rather be hard. Sometimes you're cool when you'd rather be hot. But you'd rather be cool than be what you're not.

Z knows his mojo is working. Good, he thinks, because it's

got a lot of work to do. Z starts singing. His mojo is swinging.

It dawns on Z that with Velva he has lost the love of his life only an instant after discovering it. He knows he'll never find the likes of it again. Love is part of the software. Grief overwhelms him like a tidal wave. Grief is part of the software.

That evening the moon rises full. Something stronger than Z pulls him out into the night. Staring up at the moon, he feels a strange birth stirring in his gut. His feelings tear loose in a wild scream of grief. Again and again he screams and howls at the moon, his face a cascade of tears. He feels as though his howling will tear him open. Z is giving birth to himself.

This is when Z discovers his affinity with the moon and becomes the Wolfman. He is initiated into the pack by the spirit of the DJ, Wolfman Jack, in a blood ceremony whose details I am not at liberty to divulge. It consists of rubbing pricked thumbs together to show no one has ZITS.

Z's first assignment is the mass murder mess. His end you know. He will not be the last to go. Suffice it to say that there are many of us and we know how to recognize one another. The young ones are noble and savage, the old ones are cranky, stubborn and foolish.

The pack understands that in America we have to move beyond the intelligence. The pack understands that the intelligence could guide one in the relatively simple conditions of the old country, but that the intelligence is not intelligent enough to deal with conditions in America. Not intelligent enough and not moving enough. Because where the old country was relatively static, America above all has to move or die. And the pack understands that the only intelligence intelligent enough to move beyond the intelligence is the intelligence of music. It is the only intelligence that is obtuse enough. That moves enough. Because you have to move it move it move it. Groove it groove it groove it. Repose yourself. Depose yourself. Expose yourself.

Ladies and gentlemen, take my advice. Pull down your pants and slide on the ice. Put another nickel in, in the nickelodeon, it's music, music, music.

Datta. Yatta. Datta.
Yaddadadadada.
Shanty, shanty, shanty,
Down in shanty town.

SHANTY SHANTY SHANTY

ShaNTy ShaNTy

SNT

S^NT>

S^NT>

S^NT>>>>>>>>>>>>>>>>>><

<~~~~~~----------____________________

: : : : : : : : : : : : : : : : : : : >>>>>

=================>>>>>>>>>>>>>#^\+#*<<<<<<<<<<<<<<=================

{+M+}

M^MM<

M^MM<

<<<<<<<<<<<<<<M^MM<

MMM

MuMMy MuMMy

MUMMY MUMMY MUMMY

a mummy's curse}************************+++++++++++===-->

Some encounters leave you amused and satisfied, others puzzled and amazed. This is a story about being puzzled and amazed.

Anyway, my reaction when I first saw Vermeer's *View of Delft* at the Hague was dissatisfied and puzzled. I remember thinking, Yeah, it's a nice painting, but what's all the fuss about? That was twenty years ago, so the fact that I remember seeing it and remember feeling dissatisfied and puzzled already says something. Still, my feelings these days tend to the uncharitable when it comes to European so-called high culture. When high culture is invoked I always think of Beethoven as interpreted by the Auschwitz Philharmonic.

I'd been eager for another look at the *View of Delft* because of a story told me by a painter friend. He explained how a guard in the Maruithuis Museum, evidently noticing his interest in the painting, closed the drapes to one side of it so that the room became quite dark. And my friend was amazed to see that the painting apparently glowed with its own light.

For some reason, this story reminded me of an experience I had in the shadowy Temple of Osiris up the Nile in Egypt. I was lamenting the circumstance that it was too dark to observe the paintings and hieroglyphs on the walls, when I saw a guide grab a tourist's guide book, open it up, and catching what little light there was on the white of the printed page, focussed it on the walls with sufficient luminosity to make out the murals. That's what I call a good guide book. It's still the best example I know of writing illuminating a work of art.

As I say, these days high culture sometimes seems to me nothing but a classy conspiracy in the service of an oppressive elite. But I was hardly prepared for what the storyteller Willem de Ridder told me in a conversation we had in the Kyzer cafe in Amsterdam. His contention is that not merely culture, but language itself is a conspiracy to suppress and control the masses. And he has proof. De Ridder explained how the Church had imposed Latin on the native tongues of Europe, giving us the European languages that we have today. But traces of an ur-language remain as a kind of code which when deciphered yields a lingua franca inseparable from the body and its physical existence, as opposed to the abstractions in which we communicate now.

Not that I'm against abstractions. On the contrary. Increasing abstraction facilitates transmission of more data and so gets closer to experience. The more abstract the more concrete. Someone has said that the problem with D.H. Lawrence's *Lady Chatterly* was that it wasn't obscene enough. The problems we have in formulating and transmitting actual experience is that we aren't yet abstract enough.

When we are abstract enough we may find that code, the ur-language, urging us to merge with the ur-matter, at the level of interaction where matter is merely a matter of mergings and emergings.

But there's a trade-off, according to Lawrence. "Understand less transmit more," he said. The problem is he didn't sufficiently follow his own advice. He was sick with the need to understand everything, or to understand everything in a certain compartmental way. Like the rest of us. Lawrence understood this. "Understanding is not the artist's job," he said. "In that sense," he said, "there's less distance between an artist and a coal miner than between an artist and an intellectual. I'm speaking of artists of all kinds, including writers. Especially writers."

"How can you use language without understanding it?" I asked.

"Everyone uses language without understanding it," Lawrence said. "We just make that clear."

Lawrence handed me a sheet of paper, actually it was a photocopy.

v^^* #+#* %%% @&<.> #~~@#* <<-{&+* ::

|.|=~~ _-._ ~+|++/+='=''==* \\/'-% ../@//\~)&[^

/%\%|: -_-'^#//=]<*>{:*

'"'%% ='=/+ (^~~~\\|-_-":+* }""_-/='* }{.%/--*

"This was found in the Temple of Osiris in Egypt," he said. "Abydos. The interesting thing about it is it isn't Egyptian, you see. It's not hieroglyphic, it doesn't correspond to anything we know about ancient languages. Except that it is a language. But maybe a language that can't be translated, do you follow? Couldn't be translated even if we understood it."

"I don't understand."

"You don't need to understand. Not in the way you

understand it," said Lawrence. "You need to understand that understanding is an interruption. Understanding is always an interruption of what you understand in the form of the cryptic. You need to interrupt yourself. What you need to do is go to Egypt, to the tombs of Luxor, to visit the crypt and see for yourself. Because it can't be translated."

A report from Luxor actually exists, so obviously he went, even though we know nothing about the circumstances. It was written in the form of notes, often incoherent, which we will have to interpret. Internal manuscript evidence suggests he was on the edge. Malaria? Nervous breakdown? Brain damage? No way of knowing.

He described the hotel where he was staying. *An old colonial establishment overlooking the Nile, high ceilings, white-washed walls, slow ceiling fans, long windows opening to balconies from which you can see the Valley of the Kings across the river vibrating in the heat.* At the end of the corridor outside the room sat a tall Black man in flowing white galabia and head dress, imperturbable, waiting. *This man both pleases and frightens me. What is he waiting for? Of course he's a servant waiting for requests for service. At the same time, it's clear he's waiting for something else.*

What seemed to unnerve him, as far as we can tell, was the feeling that the tall black man was waiting for the same thing he himself was waiting for. That we're all waiting for. Because isn't that what's unnerving all of us? That we know everything is unstable, that we know it's got to change, but we don't know how, where or when. *When I look at the landscape out the window, the broad Nile with its lateen sails, its white steamers at the dock, the green fertile riversides and the barren hills beyond shivering in the heat, Egypt, all of it a great trembling sphinx-like beast, sick and dormant, but quivering with menace, I think of New York, of London, of Paris. Underneath the febrile activity the same stasis. The same slow rot. The same menace.* There follows some notes on possible meanings of "sphinx," not relevant here. Mostly in the nature of the Sphinx as sphincter, holding things back. We don't claim to understand.

He went to the tombs in the Valley of the Kings across the river. His only notation afterward: *more stasis. The hieroglyphic pictograms came after the beginning of abstract writing as we know it, replacing it. Fascinating. And once replacing became set. As if in concrete. Set. One of the gods.*

But his take on Karnak was another story.

Karnak he considered crushing. *The giant Sequoias in California, roots like gargantuan feet whose legs you can only see the lower part of before they disappear in a cover of foliage, implying colossi hovering above. So here the massive pillars, scale off the chart, invoking presence of crushing deities, merciless, to whom we are as ants. Dwarfed, I think is the word. Do not dare to resist. Anything.*

He must have asked too many questions, though. Of someone. The fundamentalists were already yapping regularly in the mosques, religion and revolution. He'd been befriended by a Copt, evidentally, with whom he was perhaps too often seen. The Copts were not popular it seems with the government, as Christians less so with the fundamentalists. Coming out from under one of the monstrous vaults he suddenly saw a hundred dollar bill on an intricate mosaic floor and sidestepped quickly to pick it up. Where he had just been a huge rock shattered on the ground. Stepping back under the vault, almost fainting, he noted that the rock was not of the material of which the ruins consisted. And that the hundred dollar bill was not there, nor the mosaic, he must have hallucinated.

That was his first, you might say, rock hard evidence of Total Control, Inc. activity, though he didn't at the time recognize it. He went back to the hotel to get ahold of himself and to pass the hours of maximum heat in the cool white-wash of his room. The number in the white galabia was waiting at the end of the hall.

That afternoon he went to the Luxor Museum. He was surprised to see how small it was, nor did he realize before-hand that it was dedicated to the reign of Akhnaton. What quickly impressed him was that though it was a small museum, each item seemed to flame with the inner luster of a gem. Akhnaton was not popular with the priests, he learned. The priests had conceived the gods as a divine bureaucracy, a heavy-handed but effective way to impose their priestocratic control on the country. Akhnaton, as everyone knows, was the pioneer monotheist—read, an attempt to clean out an oppressive polytheistic bureaucracy that required multiple departments of everything with their hives of sub-departments and proliferating agencies. The priests hated Akhnaton so much that when he died and they regained control, they obliterated every vestige of his reign, the sculpture, the painting, the monotheistic capital city he had built. Of the scattered remains, everything obtainable had been collected in this small museum, he discovered.

He quickly observed that everything in the museum was distinguishable at a glance from the usual overbearing, dead magnificence of ancient Egyptian art. Each piece was in-vested with a dazzling individuality, each individual a dis-tant simulacrum of the One, each unique and unlike any other. In the few cases where two pieces represented the same theme he saw that they were nevertheless completely different.

These sculptures, it says in his notes, *this must have been what Lawrence meant. These artifacts articulate a language, a language we don't understand, a cryptic language we don't need to understand until it interrupts, a language that understands us. The opposite of the Sphinx.* I'm not sure I understand. Again: *Windows to allness.* Again: *The riddle of the Sphinx is why it needs to riddle, to hold things back.*

It was in the museum, apparently, that he first met Dr. Ahfug. The stolid, swarthy, fez-wearing Ahfug, as I have reason to know, is not exactly a crowd pleaser. In fact he emanates what you might call a negative charisma, a species of psychological B.O. The sole direct reference reads, *It's not on the basis of his personal charm that I agreed to meet Ahfug tonight in the bazaar.*

From the police reports we know that this Ahfug persuaded him to cross the Nile, at night, to visit one of the tombs to which the Dr. (of what?) had access, apparently, when he liked. We know also that this tomb had some particular association with the ancient god Set. I don't know how much you know about Set, the dog-faced god. He was a god of war, of power, of control. More about this later. But one thing: don't imagine that because he was an ancient god, Set has lost his potency. The gods are always with us in one form or another. Your only defense is to ignore them. Don't make the mistake of getting involved in things you know nothing about.

We also know that locally there is a curse connected with this tomb. Why this tomb, nobody seems to know. The story is that on certain days of the year people disappear there, never to be seen again—most notorious being the case of a young female archeology student, whose blond body was never found.

And in fact he was never seen again either.

When I got to Luxor I made a point of staying in the same room in the same hotel. And, of course, through contacts I arranged to meet the mysterious Dr. Ahfug.

"Let's not beat around the bush, Ahfug," I told him. "We want to know what happened to our boy."

"That is something I cannot tell you," Ahfug said. "But I can take you to someone who can. You will have to come with me." There was something disconcerting about Ahfug's eyes. After a while I realized what it was. He never blinked.

"If you think I'm going anywhere with you, you're rifling the wrong tomb."

I had weighed my words carefully, wanting to clue him that we knew more about him than he might think. He got the message all right, but again, he didn't blink.

"I am an antiquities dealer," he said. "And about coming with me, you shall change your mind."

He clapped his hands. We were sitting in the bar of the hotel, late at night, and we were the only customers. I expected to see a waiter respond with the bill, but instead, out of an obscure doorway, a young woman emerged, slim, blond, walking carefully as if among invisible obstacles. I say slim, but what immediately struck me since she was wearing a short skirt and an almost absurdly tight sweater was that, despite her slender build she was extremely voluptuous. I couldn't believe she was wearing clothing that vulnerable to the tendency among Arab men to consider Western women whores to begin with. But it wasn't only her flimsy clothing, it was some way she had of moving, something in her eyes that suggested invasion, violation.

"This is Daisy," said Ahfug. "She was with your friend during the night you are interested in. Say hello to the gentleman, Daisy."

"Hello, sir," said Daisy.

"Only Daisy knows what happened that night," said Ahfug. "Sit, Daisy."

Daisy sat down.

"Well, what happened," I asked. I noticed that her blue eyes were opened wide, her pupils enlarged. Then I realized that she too never blinked.

"He disappeared," said Daisy.

"We know that. How?"

"Sir, I was there but I can't describe it. There are those who can. I can only show you the place." Her voice was monotone, rhythmless.

"Why can't you describe it?"

"Because you won't believe me. I wouldn't even know how to begin. And besides, it's unspeakable."

That's why I finally decided to go with them. I knew it was a risk, but sometimes you have to take risks. First I went up to my room and got rid of pocket litter, as we call it, anything that might get me into trouble. Then I pocketed my piece and went back down. My friend in the white galabia was in the corridor, waiting.

You got into the boat with the triangular lateen sail down at the pier, but as soon as the boat moved away from the lights of Luxor it was dark as black velvet. You were midstream before you noticed that the boat was not heading for the landing of the Valley of the Kings but was angling upstream.

Soon the small crew was using oars to make headway against the current. I wonder if you had foreseen that, that feeling that you get when the situation suddenly moves beyond your control, into unknown territory, your fate in the keeping of persons of dubious character, and there's nothing you can do about it.

You probably landed upstream close enough to the Valley of the Kings to double back to one of the outlying tombs. Or was it a tomb we don't know about? Dr. Ahfug, in custody, claimed that it was the girl who was in control of him and not the other way around, as it must have appeared to you.

We know that they led you in to the tomb of some king or other, though probably by this point you were already wondering whether it wasn't going to be yours. What happened to you next was not so much unbelievable as it was ambiguous. Probably even you didn't know what to think about it. If you were thinking at all. We've finally concluded that nothing we can say about it is true. But we can speculate. And from what little information we have try and put it together.

They say that Akhnaton's efforts aside, Osiris was the closest thing they had in Egypt to a humane god, one with redemptive qualities that may be the source of later western deities personifying regeneration and therefore, simply, hope. Rather than hopeless oppression. To achieve this status he first had to die, killed by his evil brother Set. In other words, to represent hope, he first of all had to not be there, which is logical, since you don't hope for something you have, only for something that you don't.

When they took you into the tomb, your hands bound behind you, you were of course confronted with the servant in the white galabia. Only it turned out that what he was a servant of was of the god Set. The minute they led you into the mummy's chamber you saw it all, it was obvious. The lid, or rather lids, because there were several, were already off the sarcophagus, and you could see the loose, papery wrappings by the flickering illumination of the red torchlight. And you knew that you had to confront that which, at bottom, all of us dread the most—the Mummy's Curse. Because we all understand, at heart, that the mummies that bring us into the world simultaneously doom us to departure from it. The Mummy's Curse leads to the crypt. No escape. So you probably knew that you were finally facing the thing itself.

What followed was in all likelihood very uncouth. It was probably then that they stripped you naked with your legs and arms spread. It was probably then also that the girl came out in her Isis costume and did her dance. We conclude this on the basis of the Polaroid shots we recovered. Apparently she danced while the white galabia, his robes gathered up at the loins, played the ritual tennis game with the Set figure. The last snap has the scoreboard showing game, Set, match. We think that tennis worked its way into the ritual due to colonial influences. Sports, you know, are not simply the domain of jocks. Sports have a profound religious root, which explains their wide popular appeal. A culture without sports is a culture without gods and heroes. In any case, it certainly could have been on that last, game ending-shot when you realized you had met your fatal match.

Yes, your fate. You were chosen. First drugged, then injected with the holy aphrodisiac. At least this is what we think. Because we've been able to trace your deposit in the sperm bank. It was made under the name of O. Serious, but it was you all right, we know because analysis proved the genetic material was identical. And because every withdrawal was made in the name of I. Seize. Read: I, Sis, because traditionally she was your sister and your spouse.

Madness. All right, madness. We go even further, we agree it was madness. Which doesn't mean it didn't happen, does it? Nor does it bring you back. Henceforth you are known only by your absence. Which has its advantages, as of course you know, knew all along. That there is far more power in an oneiric absence than in an onerous presence. And so, the mystic Tagger, the unknown grafitti soldier.

And here we think we can tentatively make the connection with the more recent international deathcult of the Sphinx, or the Iron Sphincters as they are known in Germany. A.k.a. up-tight assholes, alias neonaziskin heads. Of course the neonazis' kin are monolith bureaucracies anywhere, anytime, and their always attendant conscientious resenters. But the neonaziskins are special, even as resenters, especially thick-skinned, and skulled, always sure to do the dirty work of the masters they rebel against, in this case the top secret omnibureaucracy of Total Control, Inc. They push their presence on us, yes, the neoskins, as supremacists, as knownothings, as fundamentalists of all sorts. But the Sphinx is anal-retentive. She holds things back. Her sign is static. Mere interference. Interruption. And you can't jam the airways one hundred percent of the time. The ponderous walls of Karnak are insufficient to keep it out. Something is going to slip through. It doesn't matter what. The tiniest lapse, the least hint of another way, another mentality, another world is enough. The reaction is always, we want more. It doesn't even matter that we'll never get it.

The Iron Sphincters are able to keep things in indefinitely, until what should come out their assholes comes out somewhere else—out their mouths, for example, or the barrels of their guns. But because of the affair down in Luxor we were tuned in, and we were able to decipher some information through the garble of static passing through the Lebanese-Bavaria channel of the terrorist network, Beirut to Bayreuth. In short, we came to suspect that they were planning an attempt on the Anne Frank House.

And that is why we found traces of your absence in the Netherlands. The Netherlands. Think about it. Nether. As in netherworld. It is well known that Osiris, after being murdered and dismembered by his brother Set, after the pieces of the corpse were thrown into the Nile, after they were found by his sister Isis, after the pieces came together again and he resurrected, he became lord of the netherworld and judge of the dead. Judge of the dead. Absent from the living.

But an absence like light. Invisible, but making everything else visible. So, associated with Ra, the sun. Like Akhnaton's one sun god, latent and potent. Overcome at night, rising again each day. Judge of the dead who judge the living. Ra. Ra Ra. Which is why we decided to visit the Hague again to view the *View of Delft*. To see the invisible.

Our contact in the Netherlands was Ihab, about whom we knew nothing except he was an Arab. We were directed to a poor, distant, mostly Arab suburb of Amsterdam, but not to an address. To a car. To a red Jaguar convertible, exactly, which in fact we found easily enough, since it was parked in an impoverished street inhabited, it appeared, mostly by thugs, whores, pimps and petty criminals, including, no doubt, any number of car thieves. There it was at the curb, mint new, red, empty, top down, door ajar and motor running. Ihab nowhere evident.

Then a stunning Oriental woman in a red dress rippled into the car and arranged herself in the shotgun seat. We noticed to one another that they both had beautiful bodies, she and the car.

"Ybod quali itspir," said someone behind us, "as our poet writes." A darkish fellow with curly close-cropped hair. "I am Ihab."

"What does it mean?"

"It means body equals spirit. More I cannot tell you. La'al Verlin is our national poet. He has a way of turning the banal into the divine—or at least the imponderable. 'Ertin combees namdynic,' as he says."

"To which side of the language conspiracy does he aspire?" we asked.

"You mean conspire."

"Either way."

"And is he a good guy or a bad guy?"

"Verlin is a language liberator. That's what a poet is."

"And what about your side?"

He lifted his eyebrows one by one. "My side is what the poet calls 'ibblevisin.' "

"Meaning?" we asked.

"We go to see," he answered. A taxi drove up, we followed the red car through the Netherlands, into the center of Amsterdam, into its netherworld.

Ihab directed us into the red light district of Amsterdam, its tough sailor bars and store front whore houses, the women in garter belts and sleazy underwear, more or less naked, exhibiting sad, sagged figures behind plate glass windows like tired mannequins. Then we went around a corner into a narrow street where the women in the windows were as if from another world. In fact, they were from another world, the far east, with perfect bodies, nude, nothing between your eyes and their golden thighs but your imagination. Their cold eyes, glassy, ices, stared beyond you as each maintained her motionless pose, Venus in stasis.

Later that same day, via Ihab—and it's hard to believe this was mere coincidence—we met the woman known as "the Happy Hooker." She did seem to be happy, intent on it even, brushing aside anything negative, a rotund, vivacious woman, very quick, energetic, affable, dynamic, Aphrodite in action. She seemed perpetually in motion even when still. It was clear she liked sex. Maybe that's what made her happy. She insisted on showing us around Amsterdam, and in conversation it turned out that she was a Jew who was confined to a concentration camp in the far east as a child. Maybe that's why she she was always moving. Maybe moving made her happy. As a certain monotheist, not Akhnaton, said down in Egypt Land, My people, let's go. Or as the poet Verlin once put it, "Gets let a voomon."

In fact, they moved. Ihab provided the contacts and they moved quickly. Their report, some of it garbled, most of it notes since they didn't have time to finish, obviously, records the encounter with Tagger.

In Rembrandt's old neighborhood, the ancient Jewish ghetto, confined by poverty and alienation. Why so many of his models look unDutch.

And the subsequent visit to the Anne Frank House.

After Ahfug turned up. Tagger on his tail. Emerging from oneiric absence.

Meeting Tagger thrown out of bar in whore district. Gets up off sidewalk: "I'm Tagger."

Following Ahfug since Cairo, via Bayreuth and the Wagner festival. "Almost suffocated by the Ring Cycle, escaped by motorcycle, heavy stuff. Sits on the spirit like konigsbergerklops on the stomach. Ahfug goes every year, meets his Nazi amigos. The key is in Delft."

Constipated Nazi Sphinx stasis. Unholy whole.

Confined to the secret apartment, they were constrained to stay still. In those circumstances only the spirit could move. Twenty-five months. How not to suffocate.

Particularities. The clippings tacked to wall, newspaper photos. Baby pictures, family photos, girl book illustration. Impressionist reproduction, Rodin. Hollywood glamor stars, the little map with pins showing Allied progress against Nazis, almost to Amsterdam. What was there was what wasn't there. Doublevision. Spirit binoculars.

New revelation. Tagger's a cryptographer, that's why he's on the case.

Breakthrough: Tagger at Anne Frank House suddenly realizes he's been to house not once but twice. Tagger staggered. The second time when it was already a monument, but also once before. Then he remembers going to the shabby door which opened into a bare wooden room. There a man sat at a desk grinding a lens. "What do you expect to see?" Tagger asked. "Nature naturing," the man said. "Sight seeing. The visible invisibling." This is what you now see scribbled on walls everywhere, of course, something started by Tagger. It was only much later that he learned about Spinoza, spending his life invisibled in Amsterdam, grinding lenses. This memory is like a mystic experience, he says. Like going from telescope to binoculars, it fills out the picture. More to point, it gives him the lens to decode the coded message secretly copied by the Mossad in Ahfug's hotel room. Doublevision. To decode doubletalk.

' " '%% ='=/+ (^~~~\\|-_-":+* }""_-/='* }{.%/--*

He was able to decode the answer. But, not the question, was the problem. And then not the whole answer, only parts.

Part of the answer was: "Nature nature. See sight. Only the invisible makes visible."

It was then, then. The second time. That he walked into the secret room. The secret room off the secret room. The man was bent over a microscope, working on something with a dissecting tool. He looked up: "You see? You cut and you cut, and finally there is nothing there. And when there is finally nothing there," he waved his hand around, "it is everywhere."

I checked this out when I got to Delft. I was puzzled and amazed. Sure enough, *A View of Delft* is not a view of Delft. It's a painting of something not there, that's what's so extraordinary. It's a painting of light, of the invisible. The first time I saw it I couldn't see it because I only saw what was visible. That sounds complicated. But once you see it's a picture of seeing it's so simple.

As a result of this investigation, Ahfug was exposed, and then invisibled. Thanks to Tagger, the Anne Frank House is still there. The cost: the wipeout of Ihab and his group by an Iron Sphincter assassination team, and an incomplete report. The benefit: to be assessed by future generations.

-_-

~_~ ~|~ *_*

"_"

/*\ /%/

('=')

:|({[/_ ~-=*+#<

oO0Oo

-o+O+o-

v^^* #+#* %%% @<.> #~~@#* <<-{&+* ::
|.|=~~ _-._ ~+|++/+='=''==* \\/'-% ../@//\~)&[^
/%\%|: -_-'^#//=]<*>{:*
'"'%% ='=/+ (^~~~\\|-_-":+* }""_-/='* }{.%/--*

50,010,008}}}}}}}}}}}}}))))))>>>>>/////////%%%%%%%%::::===>

You know what I hate? People who wear trade marks on their clothes. As if to say you are what you buy. But hey, do it yourself. Make up your own mark. Make a statement. Write yourself in to the book of life.

It's happening. I see signs everywhere. They are signs that say, "Hey, I'm me. Pay attention." And the reason is is that nobody is.

It's true I'm sensitive to style. Especially in clothes. Even for a woman, I mean. Because I'm in modes. But this is not a fad. This is a movement. I call it Egoslogan. A movement about persons. But it's not exclusive. It includes second persons and third persons as well as first persons. It's just, like, intensely personal.

I saw a T-shirt the other day that said, "I'm On Hold." It was on an older woman, maybe pushing sixty, which gave it a kind of twist. Then I saw one on a young woman that said "Handle With Care." That was over her breasts, which were big and bouncy. On her back it said, "This Side Up." She was with a big, strong guy whose chest said, "Agile."

Egoslogan.

In the state where I live residents worried about too many people moving in started using bumper stickers that said "Native." Soon bumper stickers appeared that said "Alien," others that said "Naive." Another series began when religious types started sticking "I Found It" on their bumpers. A sticker immediately appeared saying "I Lost It," and another saying "Keep It." In California where things often get started people have long since used their license plates to declare identity rather than acquiesce in anonymity. "I 1 BB ME." "4Q." "I M A QT." "U R 2 MUCH." "Y W8." "OVER 8." "E Z." "WHO 1."

Graffiti is Egoslogan in a different kind of writing, writing that can skip language. And it can skip countries. It's spread to France where they call it "le tagging." What's it all about? Maybe people anymore don't want to be the blank page for other people. Maybe people want a clean slate. To write their own things, the first of which is "I exist." Or maybe, like animals, they need to mark a territory, tagging it with a signature.

But really there are a lot of people who don't exist. Living, breathing people, some of whom have just slipped between the cracks and there are more and more of those, but also plenty of people who go to work every day, who have bank accounts, relatives, social networks, families, boyfriends or girlfriends, some of them even raise children, belong to the P.T.A. It's not they aren't alive, it's that they don't exist. They don't count. Ask them.

Even so, I'm beginning to find traces of them. More and more evidence that they're crawling out from under whatever. Rocks, old newspapers, tupperware, corporate desks. And this urge to make your mark, to create a signature, is maybe not even so new. I was recently at the Maruithuis museum in the Hague, and found a painting of a church interior by G. Houhgiest, 1600-1661, featuring in the foreground a pillar prominently marked by grafitti.

I totally agreed with her. About the concept of Egoslogan I mean. I first noticed signs in Spain and southern France. There's a long tradition there of people living in caves, and some people still do. Troglodytes, they're called. They go way back to the Stone Age and from the very beginning they were painting cryptic symbols on their walls which to this day remain indecipherable, even to anthropologists.

I forgot to mention, I'm an anthropologist. Well, more an anthroapologist, I try to find excuses for the existence of the human race. Maybe that's why I'm not particularly mystified by the cave paintings, the gorgeous ones at Lascaux, for example. They are clearly the works of persons who wanted to affirm their existence.

I exist. That's not such a simple proposition, when you think about it. To be alive is one thing. To exist, to count for something, is another.

The first really exciting clue I found was written on a fragment of old envelope I picked up in a Poste de Télégram et Télégraphe in Paris. The writing was smudgy, as if written with a soft, ill sharpened pencil. It said: /*\. &/%/. -- oO0Oo.

Doodling, you say. Maybe. But even assuming it's doodling, that doesn't mean it's beside the point. Doodling is a kind of play. But when you start talking about play, how far are you from a form of meditation, for example? And in fact how far from meaning can any mental activity ever get?

Because certainly any kind of expressive artifact is the result of mental activity, whether it succeeds in communicating or not.

But whether it succeeds in communicating or not is exactly the question. /*\. &/%/. --oO0Oo. To me, that looks like an effort by somebody to express something. The open truncated pyramid of the first symbol with a star inside—is that not as much as to express a state of potential, of something contained and held back but ready to take off, to explode, maybe volcanically? Then the ampersand followed by the musical arrangement of oughts and slashes—is that not a sign of what would follow the eruption, a high, followed by a low, ending with a gesture of hope? And then the two dashes followed by every possible variation of nothing, a declaration of nullity, but at the same time nullity arranged with careful symmetry, nullity anulled. Becoming eggs of possibility. A sort of signature. And maybe also, in its rise and fall as the vowel of exclamation, of surprise, an exclamation of discovery, of perhaps insight.

Be that as, as they say, it may, it was only the beginning. No doubt I would have forgotten all about it had it not been for a visit from an artist friend who was engaged in a project to create a new universal alphabet, as she put it. To tell the truth, I

but it got me to thinking. Maybe there's a richer alphabet hidden in the signs and symbols thrown off by the daily evolutions of the world.

Take   Lake Country in England before you write off Wordsworth. Once there you'll understand that he was merely making a long transcription of what he read in the landscape. Go to the Lochs of Scotland, with their misty presences. Or the Dordogne in the Midi of France, haunted by Cro-Magnon as Henry Miller was quick to pick up from the feel of the countryside.

But the great earth opus in the Midi, rivalling the visual odes of Lascaux, is the inhuman iconography of little known l'Aven d'Armand, the work of millions of years of millions of sulphurous dribbles scribbling a vast subterranean epic. This is the year 50,010,008, according to a fellow anthroapologist, dating on a straight incremental basis from the end of the Ice Age rather than the usual before and after of Christian culture. If so, l'Aven d'Armand must have been writing itself from the year zero, judging by

With the tremendous size of its single chamber, into which you could fit a fleet of Colosseums, all of it structured like some immense Piranese ruin made of gargantuan vaults and stalactic columns, and embellished with extravagant colors and runic elaborations taking on different forms and degrees of complication depending on whether you're observing them close up or from the vast heights and distances possible in the cavern, you have the impression when you first see it of an involuted and barbaric articulation shaped like the inside of your brain. The straggled trains of tourists circulating through l'Aven along the marked paths or on the wooden stairways leading from one level to another seem lost and astray, reduced by sheer volume of space to insignificance. It was in this scene out of Dante's hell that I first became aware of

Anthroapology could be considered a forensic science. The

a mummy for example requires deductive

a detective to identify a corpse

and the circumstances of its demise. Even the decoding of mysterious inscriptions has strong whodunnit elements. So when I wandered off the

v^^* #+#* %%% @&<.> #~~@#* <<-{&+* ::
|.|=~~ _-._ ~+|++/+='=''==* \\/'-% ../@//\~)&[^
/%\%|: -_-'^#//=]<*>{:*
'"'%% ='=/+ (^~~~\\|-_-":+* }""_-/='* }{.%/--*
inscribed carefully in the soft rock, the letters being about two centimeters high, with margins approximately a half a meter apart. Luckily I had a camera with a flash.

thoroughly consulted the literature. Nothing. Attempts at dating were futile in the absence of further information. Given the conditions inside the cavern it could

or from yesterday. But clearly an intelligence

since as yet I had told no one, though I suppose from my inquiries someone could have pieced it together. He implied sources of information. I didn't trust him. But then I suppose he didn't trust me. In any case the chance to investigate a possible source of macrochromatics in microcosm was too tempting. It went off my chromatic scale. So to

sewers and catacombs under Paris as nothing in extent compared to the honeycomb of old quarries long since abandoned, covered over or otherwise lost. It was through these that he proposed to conduct me. I had heard stories of cocksure students embarked in them on a dare lost for days or never

In fact he was never seen again. Of course you know that, but I'm not writing this only for you. I'm writing it as a form of protection in case of double cross, blackmail or planned misadventure. Of course you know that too. You know this isn't the unique copy and you know that in the end this will be published somewhere. You know and you know. It's what you don't know that interests me. It's only when I know what you don't know that I'll know what you know.

You know that what you call the translations were in verse, not prose, apparently unrelated to the original photograph. You know that no one was able to find the inscription in the cave again. Possibly forged,

You never met him. None of you. He wasn't an impressive specimen, though there was something about him. Something that didn't add up, or that added up to more than it should have. How can I put it? He looked like a nerd but there was something urgent about him that was impressive. A defrocked professor of archeology who long ago missed his chance for tenure because of his batty theories. Mainly that all the major changes in the evolution of life on earth were caused by catastrophic cataclysms, was the way he liked to refer to them. Some originating in outer space, some in the bowels, as they say, of the earth. He was on the track of something big and you knew it. What he called the revolt of the chromos. I mean, what the hell is that? If you know you're not telling me about it.

And I suspect you do know. I mean that's your business, isn't it? That I'm in over my head is an understatement. But you wanted someone in over his head, didn't you? Because if one weren't in over one's head one wouldn't have signed on. Would one.

He liked to babble about chromatic scales. At first I thought he was talking fish. Or maybe weight. But it wasn't either of those. He knew I didn't follow but he babbled anyway, who knows why.

I know it had to do with the spread of strange viral diseases, proliferation and metamorphosis was the way he put it. Obviously the first thing I had to do was head for the morgue. But I did a little research in front. I found that the chromatic scale refers to notes not included in the regular diatonic scale. I mean, I don't know anything about music, but chromatics seem to involve notes between notes, notes that though normally left out can be used to complicate and enrich the normal scale with subtle ambiguities, the flats and sharps, the subtle ambiguities beyond normal perception that actually make up most of our experience even though we can't rationally account for them. Or am I overstating the case? Should I just say, black keys? And anyway, what did that have to do with strange viral diseases?

Harry, at the morgue, was not helpful, even though he was probably still drinking the last fifth of Makers Mark I slipped him. I was left with toe tags that indicated natural causes and a look they all seemed to have on their faces that implied they were glad to get it over with. All seventeen of them. And this was only one morgue, they were on ice all over the city, but the newspapers hadn't put two and two together yet and officialdom was intentionally slow to react before they knew what they were dealing with. If it ever worried about anything the multinational that started all this was probably shitting green, and I guarantee I wasn't the only agent in the field.

That was when I called you to say that I thought this thing was bigger than you thought and you said that you always thought it was bigger than you thought. You told me to hop the next Concorde for Europe and I said this was really starting to cost and you said you were paying the bills.

At Heathrow I rented a car and drove up to Oxford, as directed. It was interesting to see Oxford, a whole tradition frozen in stone, very esthetic. It reminded me of an old wedding cake—desiccated but beautiful. I wished I'd had time for some tourism. Okay I'm a shammus but I'm a sensitive shammus. If you puzzle me do I not think? If you hassle me do I not get pissed? Next stop Stratford.

But you know as well as I do that I was both puzzled and hassled at this point. Because the

already dead. And the letter didn't mention that when I knocked on his door I would immediately become a suspect. Especially when they began checking

to me this will tell the story. Every day I put one copy in the mail to a safe place and one to you just so you know what

At Oxford I   dignified servant

ancient Balliol   . He wouldn't tell me who

small package. After

encased a small hollow bird's egg, obviously fragile but almost whole, brown freckles on light blue. The note with it said that the egg was picked up on the grounds of Wordsworth's house in the Lake Country, in the gardens he designed, and that the freckles could be read as a message from Wordsworth himself

if   .   Obviously   an egg of possibility. Where had I heard that phrase before?

After much   help of a Lecturer

decoded egg. Meanwhile,   insinuating   my dead contact   . This took weeks. During which time I was under constant surveillance by Scotland Yard.

his hands

on the girl's breasts. As my companion said, an odd sort of inspector indeed. But the girl seemed to mind less than we did. In fact,   . "   predicting what they're going to be attracted to," he remarked.

"Power," I suggested.

In fact, as you know, he was a person of considerable power, though who was backing him conjecture. I had my own ideas, namely . Whatever. Once bitten twice hung, as they say over here.

At first flush he didn't seem that formidable. But first of all, don't flush for everything. And then it wouldn't have surprised me if he were flushed from drinking. In any so if you have to flush twice it's a big one. That's obvious. But why am I telling you all this since obviously you know it anyway?

He thought we knew it. But actually we did not. That was the tragedy. Because there would have been so much he might have told us. Before they got to him. With the same condition he had been researching. While he was still with us, in fact, one of the models he came to admire was Hawkings. More than once he remarked to us that the more you have to say the less clearly you can say it, and that you simply have to leave it to others to decipher. And we just as often remarked that at that level it's hard to tell whether someone is saying something or saying nothing. And he just as often that in fact it was up to the listener to generate the meaning, not the speaker. And he just as often added that furthermore, come to think of it, was this not always the case?

But whether it was or not was beside the point, or at least so it seemed now. Because though death came quickly it was preceded by the gradual scrambling of the brain wires, so to speak, typical of the action of this particular virus. Gaps began appearing in his memory, larger and larger ones, though, typically, the evolution was anything but consistent. At the cybernetic level it amounted to a form of censorship, I suppose.

But all of that was incidental to the salient fact. THIS WAS THE FIRST CASE ON RECORD IN WHICH WE WERE ABLE TO DEMONSTRATE BEYOND A DOUBT THAT A HUMAN BEING COULD BE INFECTED WITH A COMPUTER VIRUS.

This we were able to ascertain after the fact, as microbe hunters. They were the ones promoting the experiment, not us. For their own evil, if purely practical, purposes.

The girl was the link. And when I say girl I mean girl. Young. Younger than her years. Later we discovered that she was actually a badly damaged Tagger. Obviously her genes had been altered for submissiveness, sexual and otherwise. And yet somehow she found a way of communicating her anguish. Somehow she had managed to find a way of telling us more than she actually knew. We don't exactly know how. Some of us think it was through body language. One researcher believes it was done via subtly modulating body odors. There is also a faction favoring psychic transmission, whatever that means. He himself speculated that she was employing a method he called chromatics.

In any case, it was through her that we arrived at the key to the whole business: what you're looking for is what you don't understand. And its corollary: if you understand it it's already been contaminated. There is already an amorphous network of egosloggers operating, however intuitively, on these principles, as anyone who carefully examines the recent explosion of Egoslogan will conclude. Because basically what we don't understand is what we are. Never mind who we are.

Once we understood these principles it did not take us long to find what they called the Factory. Factory I imagine because it was their center for neural image fabrication, viral plot production workshops and communicable conspiracy projection studios. It was also where they manufactured and bottled their bacterial nostrum, euphemistically called Simple Solution, which broke down the complexities of the genetic code into more manipulable compounds. Once we found this establishment we realized that these people did not bother with thought control, they were engaged in permanent alteration of the thought process itself. This was big. We didn't yet understand how big.

Loch Ness was also a laboratory. It was there for the most part that they researched and compiled their credulity index. The method was to construct and disseminate "true" stories with progressively elevated Gulp Ratings. The Gulp Rating apparently indicated "hard-to-swallowness," referred to by insiders simply as "lochness." Subjects were fed stories of increasing improbability until finally their gullets locked and they gagged. What they were exploiting was the basically intelligent impulse to accept the reality of something that isn't there.

We have no way of knowing whether her take on the motivation behind the project was a function of a high Gulp Rating Tolerance. Her take was that a Malthusian view of population growth had issued in a systematic attempt at population control through unleashing a humanly communicable computer virus. Other subjects of the lab's experiments actually believed that certain "underdesirable" populations were targeted for viral infection, but we had no way of knowing whether this belief was due to artificially heightened Gulp Rating Tolerances (GRTs). We did know that one of the lab's main lines of inquiry concerned the mass manipulation of GRTs. This was achieved by gradually elevating the lochness of stringently controlled information patterns.

You did not yet know that you were up against a highly organized multinational corporate effort to monopolize gene patents back to the States. in Boulder, Colorado highly classified certain Anasazi seem to predict, according to a biocybernetic inscriptions of unknown provenance, very ancient. metamorphic cybervirus that can actually think at a primitive level, thus evading There are many areas, mostly in the Southwest, with all the magic of the Dordogne, the Lake de Chelly, the Black Canyon of the Gunnison, Hopi country, Arches

White Sands, with its blinding the negative of every positive. This, of course, was where they first tested the

top secret

and at Alamagordo, the

laboratory

arch through which the empty sky stares at you, glowing red under the lid edge of Dead Horse Point, looking over the vast depth and distances, you read a scary message, and you come away feeling lucky to escape with your life.

He understood finally that there was a language he didn't understand, that none of us understood, and that there was a mechanism by which the closer you got to understanding it the less you could understand. Despite the heavy censorship exercised on the papers released by the Defense Department, he grasped, or intuited, or guessed, perceived in the very lacunae, that somehow the future is capable of affecting the present. (Of course it goes without saying that the present affects the past, this is now indisputable.) His model was basketball. We recognize, he pointed out, that sometimes we know before we shoot that the ball is going to pass through the basket, and it does. This raises the question: do we know beforehand that the ball is going to pass through the basket, or does the ball pass through the basket BECAUSE we know beforehand? But of course as his thinking about this problem advanced, his ability to think and even communicate receded. Unfortunately, because we know enough to know that herein lay the answer to how the cybervirus metamorphoses before we

we lately have come to understand that we
ourselves, maybe all of us gaps infects and
revises and possibly even the genetic code itself.
Yet this must not inhibit inquiry, and indeed should a
grammar of event syntax of elision increasingly
urgent which, because

The source of contamination the negative of every
positive—without which future
affect the present as death affects life

"How could you expect people to understand it?" the survivor said. "Or even believe it? I was there and even I don't believe it. Much less understand it. Less than you."

of every positive, the negative without which
we can't even see the positive. outside a little town in
Italy, Rimini I think it was, after a hard day of hitch hiking.
It was a long time ago, I can date it precisely from

down from the cab of the truck at a small bridge into town.
They were selling peaches by the road side, it must have been

bought a bag and sat on the stone wall of the bridge, thinking to rest and eat a peach before going into town for lunch. So I ate a peach, I can still remember the taste. It was a perfect peach, I remember thinking it was the best peach I ever ate. I threw the pit off the bridge and bit into another. I ate that one, threw the pit off the bridge and ate another. Threw the pit off the bridge and ate another. Threw the pit off the bridge and ate another. There must have been twelve or fourteen peaches in that bag and before I knew it I'd eaten them all. They were big peaches too. The Byzantine mosaics in Rimini, said to have inspired Dante, are in fact sublime.

../@//\~)&[^ v^^* #+\#* %%%* @&<.> #~~@#* |.|=~~ _-._

/'-% v^^* #+#* %%%* @&<.> #~~@#* ^\<<-{&+* :: |.|=~~

|=~~ '==* ~+|++/+='=' '==* \\/'-% . ./@//\~)&[^ /%\%|:*

-_-'^#//=]<*>{:* ' " '%% ='=/+ (^~~~\\|-_-":+* }""_-/='*

}{.%/--* %%%* _-._ ~+|++/+='=' '==* \\/'-% . ./@//\~)&[^

/%\%|:* -_-'^#//=]<*>{:* ' " '%% ='=/+ (^~~~\\|-_-":+*

}" "_-/='* }{.%/—* %%%* _-._ v^^* #+#* %%%* @&<.>

#~~@#* ^\<<-{&+* : : | . |=~~ \\/ '-% ~+|++/+='=' '==*

_-._ v^^* #^\+#* %%%* @&<.> #~~@#* #^\+#* ~+|++/

+='=' '==* \\/'-% . ./@//\~)&[^ #^\+#* %%%* @&<.>

#~~@#* ^\<<-{&+* :: | . |=~~ _-._ ~+|++/+='=''==* \/'-% ..

/@//\~)&[^ }" "_-/='* }{.%/—* %%%^* _-._ ^\<<-{&+*

: : | . |=~~ _-._ |=~~ . . /@//\~)&[^ /%\%|:* -_-'^#//=]<*>{:*

the wondering jew and the black widow murders, or the return of the planet of the apes}""""""""" ''''' ~~~~~~~~~---->

I get a strange feeling in Europe, when I go to Germany, especially, I understand that I'm already dead. In Europe I'm detached from the human race. I no longer care about sex, money, career, prestige, fun, the love of women, the admiration of men, even current events. If you come and tell me your troubles I'll sympathize, if you want to brag I'll applaud. But it's all at a remove, that is, because it moved me before,

I can go through the motions of being moved again. This is life after death. And I like it.

I probably used to be a Hamburger in some other life. Before 1939, no doubt. When I go there I feel completely at home, like a returning ghost. Maybe there was once a family branch of Hamburgers. Or maybe some adventurous ancestor calling regularly at the port to sell his wares left our genes in their pool.

Last time I was there I was walking near the port when this old fellow stopped me with a wave of his hand. It was a chilly night, chilly and damp with the cold humidity typical of certain port cities in the north of Europe that used to comprise the medieval Hanseatic League. Moisture beaded on the frigid stone and brick of the grim warehouses, chandler's shops and cheap bars that served the maritime trade. The light, billowy fog had an odd chartreuse tinge, possibly emanating from the modernistic street lamps, which also emitted a peculiar high-pitched buzz.

The old fellow tried three languages on me before he hit on English, "An English? Yes?" He spoke it fluently, with only a slight, if unfamiliar, accent. I would not have lingered except for being curious and, as I say, feeling for no justifiable reason strangely at home.

"Somebody said that the trouble with D. H. Lawrence's *Lady Chatterly* was that it wasn't obscene enough," he began. Naturally, given the Repperban, the notorious red light district near the port, I at first thought that the old man was an agent for one of the local bawdy houses. Nothing could have been further from the, as they say, truth. First of all when you really looked at the old man he wasn't really that old. He was maybe more like my age, and I'm not all that old after all. He was just care-worn, grey, burned-out and poorly dressed. Well so what, I'm care-worn, grey, burned-out and poorly dressed. Maybe that's why he singled me out. Yet there was something, I don't know, indefinably horny about this guy. You had the impression he was going to throw open his greasy trench coat and show you something you didn't want to see.

"Let me tell you a story," he continued, "and you can judge whether or not it's obscene enough."

He beckoned me into a doorway. "But first," he said, "have you seen this yet?"

He withdrew from his pocket a sheet of scrolled paper, and unrolled it in the light of the street lamp. It said:

v^^* #+#* %%% @&<.> #~~@#* <<-{&+* ::
|.|=~~ _-._ ~+|++/+='='' '==* \\/'-% ../@//\~)&[^
/%\%|: -_-'^#//=]<*>{:*
' " '%% ='=/+ (^~~~\\|-_-":+* }""_-/='* }{.%/--*

"I found this inscription near a small village in Turkey. My wife and I were there for examining a little known exquisite Greek ruins. All this was happened a long time ago. My wife was graduate student in the archeology. The site was just outside the village, but the village itself was far and away from any decent urban center. Cynthia was there for professional reason but we both thought the trip for a vacation from the long dull grinding of academic life in the States, a life that we both felt was wearing the edge of our marriage with the boring of routine. Especially sexually. Yes, Cyn was an American, about twenty-five and very cute. At least for my opinion, and not only for mine judging from the risings she always got from men no matter where we were. Cyn's archaeologist guise of thigh snug khakis and tight white T-shirt always reminded me of a sausage with tits and ass, all of which she had in great abundance, though not excess. But it was more like something about her face, her swolling lip, her pink cheek which they always looked like someone just slapped them, but more her expression than the features of themselves, of a sort of daughterly pliability want to being grown-up, maybe that was it, that made men drive up walls. And in true, she have liked men drive up walls.

"I'm occasionally Belge you see, occasionally Polish, that's why I speak English so good, but with a little indefinable accent that I can't even myself define which confuses people, maybe because myself am confused, especially about American women and how they behave, in which I never understood even though I passed many years in the States and know the statistics.

"We need money bad at the time, and since I had some connection in Istanbul, I was really thinking to take some grass or even smack out when are we going to leave, but I haven't tell Cyn about this at first because she would have to be shooked. But when I told her I think the danger kind of have turn her on. Come to think, maybe she have like to be shooked. But on seeing the inscription everything change. We are supposed experts. Then because I had thought to understand what I didn't understand from scratch. Nothing. When that happens you leave events to their intercourse.

"But first let me tell you how first we have meet. It was through Cyn's little sister.

"Sometimes I'm Jewish. Like many Jews, and some cats, I'm very curious. So this is what they mean by the wondering Jew. I'm always wondering, I wonder from one thing to the next. Once when I was Jewish I was teaching at a well-known university surrounded by cows. That was how I met Cyn's little sister. Out west is very different, starting with New Jersey. The only cows I'd seen up to then were in the Jewish

Alps, and they were tame cows. These new cows ran around by themselves and stared at you with rancid curiosity through the barbed wire of the ranch surrounding the campus. Maybe because the campus was so futuristic. At evening when I was trying to talk to one of these cows she came up to me and she loved my books. It was Cyn's little sister. At the time I was a well-known sexual anthropologist and my books were far and wide. She said she was a young student, too young for my level, but asked anyway if she could be precocious in my class.

"I was no fool. I knew there was a sex gleam in her eye. But I decided so what, if it was sex. I was new at the academic teaching, but even as I already observed, there appeared to be many a teacher fucking their student, or graduate or undergraduate even, no problem. This was before harassment, the black market of campus sex. Much done but little said, except a few cases where shit hit, as they say, fan. Some even ended in marriages.

"Of course I was already married. Later I married the little's big sister, as said. But the little was very pretty too, or sexy, like a Mack truck, in the heavy on purpose way she moved. Also smart, which was my tender spot. Brought up in the wealthy wildlife of the local posh town, with its exclusive racisms and classicisms and most was use to having her ways. As well as with her teachers.

"I once appeared as anthropologist in the schools at that high school. The Principal, after reading my books—too late—got me in his office before class.

" 'Remember,' he said, 'these are youngsters. Avoid the Big F.'

"I wasn't sure what was the Big F, but soon discovered these supposedly small rich kids had probably done it, along with everything else, some before the age of fourteen or fifteen. By sixteen, some were already trying to get straight, staying hard away from sex and drugs, or at least away from sex for drugs, with no luck. Any kid who looked straight there you probably knew was the worst. But I liked it because I too then was a rebel without pause.

"They kept inviting me to erotic joy rides by sexy teen age girls, I wondering already, what are they doing with cars, too young to drive? I don't boost on my virtue, but I never did any of these invitations. Because for a funny reason. It wasn't virtue it was I felt exploited. Besides, there are limits.

"Although at the time I had no idea what they were. So Cyn's little, used to overprivileged, I think, by the standard of normal milieux must have been a regular brat.

"But I was also a regular brat at the time. At the university were big red letters on my door saying YOU'RE DEAD! When our chairman asked what is it I told him you guys and your old boys networks. But not a conscious brat. For example I was surprised, nay offended when they didn't renew my contract. I couldn't admit a lot of things I did those days were strictly from anger. Resentence. Who can admit doing things from resentence? If you can admit it you stop doing it.

"There was no other choice, therefore, but to be a hypocrite. Though I knew, at the least, that a lot of the gross things I did were accompanied by the feeling of getting even. Getting even? With what?

"But, to continue, it wasn't long after she got into my class that we fell into bed together. Actually, what we fell into was a bush, probably sagebrush, because the campus was surrounded by chaparral and cows. So, okay. We started screwing with regulation, frequent regulation, sometimes in a bed, sometimes in a bush.

"But that's only the beginning of the story.

"The middle o: the story has unexpected developments.

"This happened when they were filming on campus one of the *Planet of the Apes* movies. It was because the campus looked so futuristic amidst of the cows and the sagebrush. All the time there were these guys in ape costumes climbing all over the university buildings, appearing into your windows when you were trying to lecture and seducing your coeds each chance they got.

"Around then I saw my little walking with an ape, his arm around her shoulder saying, 'How about meeting me at the zoo tonight, baby?'

"I have to admit, I got a little jealous. This was ape rape. Especially since she stopped coming to classes until the apes moved off locations. As usual, I was getting fond of this girl.

"After the apes were dislocated, she started coming back to class. But she had changed, I don't know if it was ape rape or the law of evolution. Now she had her own new agendas. I was now the hunted, no more the hunter. Was I ever?

"First thing, she started visiting my office before class on purpose to turn me on. But I absolutely refused to screw her before class because I didn't want to suffer the quality of my teaching. I had scruples. You may not think so and I may not think so now. But I'm not as sure as you that I'm righter now than I was then.

"What I did was restrict her to sucking my cock, making her stop before I can come. Having several advantages. First, keeping her quiet while I reviewed my notes. Second, giving a lot of energy to put into my lectures. And when we finally fell into some bush after class it was nitroglycerine.

"So that solved the problem.

"But then another problem, not so easily. She started

coming to class in manners that can only call incendiary. One day typically she would come in wearing a mini-skirt and complete see-through blouse. This bothered me because I couldn't concentrate and it rubbed the students. One Black kid, I don't know how he got there to prove things looked liberal, he couldn't believe his eyes. I thought he was going to jump on her, but no. He was piss because she was coming to class dressed as a hooker.

"This kid, he got so much piss he actually spit at her. In the middle of my lecture. Of course, everybody ignored, especially me. What would you do, as an American? I was confused, I would take any reasonable suggestion. I was piss too. After class, instead of spreading her out on my desk or disappearing with her into the underbrush I gave her a talk.

"But, 'The hell with that,' she said. 'I'm tired of hiding my sex. I don't care how men want, I want to be in front about it. To be desired. To ask for it. To be a sex object. The whole taco.'

"This was dangerous. Who's perverting who? Who's subverting who? So things petered off. She maybe was sore I didn't defend her against people spitting. But I was devoid of favoritism. A teacher has to be fair. After all.

"I realize now I didn't get it. But I still don't go get what I was supposed to get in America. However, that was a long time ago. More recently, a guy I know told me how he once literarily became a woman. Not to pretend, but literarily.

"He said this happened in Paris. He had just broken with his mistress and was very broken. One morning he woke up and he found he had become this woman, he didn't even know who she was. It wasn't his mistress. Later on he found that maybe she had once lived in the apartment where he had been living with his mistress.

"He said he was shook. Especially since she wasn't a young, sexy woman, at least, but instead an old Jewish lady. Looking in the mirror she saw all the secondary sex characteristics were gone, white stubble on the chin, and let's face it, he said, by that age it doesn't matter whether you have a vagina or a dick or both.

"In fact, he said, he didn't know why she wasn't more upset than she was. But he said that she didn't really look all that different, he'd always been prematurely grey, he'd let his hair grow long, and his cheeks were chubbier than usual because of the uncustomary French cuisine. Somebody looking at her might not be able to tell the difference, he said. And her voice sounded about the same. Actually, he said it was sort of interesting, yet, not getting into a panic.

"He said the strangest thing was she felt this overwhelming urge to talk. So much she started talking into her self, and at last became so unrested went out into the street, he said. At that point, he said, she realized that she'd come down with a bad case of—what is your word for it—logorrhea? The so-called talkies. It's happened to him before, so she comprehends there's only one way to deal, and that is to go with the flu. Better to babble to herself than to buttonhook people a la ancient marinara, freaking them out. And yet she did try to buttonhook, but they ran away. So she mentioned to first one then another, till she told all.

" 'My name was Anita,' she began. 'This was World War Two. I was a nice Jewish girl who went out of high school. Then I joined the WACS. That was the women doughboys. Nice Jewish girls didn't go in the army, even if that was where all the boys went. But I had big tits and wanted to do something with them. Yes, naive. I didn't know what I wanted.'

" 'But,' she said, 'I knew what I didn't want, and that was to be raped from my virginity by seven boys in barracks the first basic week. Then I said I was going to have a good time and what the heck. And I did, too. But I never forgot. I was going to get mine back from hell and high water.'

" 'Once they sent me to Paris near the end of the war I said here's my chance. I was in a strange foreign city full of G.I.'s and everything could happen to them. There was an underground Nazi terrorist organization that the Germans started called the Werewolves and they went around murdering people. They could think it was them. Who was to say for what if some dumb dog-face was found dead on the quai now and then on a cold misty Paris morning? But it all happened so surprising. And nothing would have happened if I hadn't met Major Moe.'

" 'Up to Moe, believe or not it, what with all the soldier boys I did with, which maybe was ten or fifteen by then, not counting the seven gang rapers, I never once had an orgasm. I didn't even know what was with an orgasm. I even went to the battalion shrink. He told me it was the familiar seven dwarf syndrome and could only be catheterized by screwing a battalion shrink seven times. But I said the hell with that, sucker.'

" 'Maybe it was the way he went about that got me so excited, Major Moe. I'm sitting in a movie when all of the sudden I feel a hand on my privates. I was a private first class and I look next to me and the hand belongs to a major. So I say, What do you think you're doing, sir? And he says, What do you think I'm doing, private?'

" 'I couldn't think of an answer to that because I knew what he was doing, so I let him do it.'

" 'When we get out of the movie it turns out he has a hotel

room, and he says, You know, private, I'm just back from the front and I love you. Why don't you come back to my hotel room?'

" 'Is that an order, sir? I ask. Because I'd never dated with anybody so highly rank.'

" 'So he says, Of course it's an order, so I say, Yes sir.'

" 'Well, Major Moe was staying at a real high-class hotel, very comfy. And the first thing he does when we get there is he orders me to take my clothes off which I do and then he sits me on a table and starts licking me, I mean you know where. That's the first time anybody ever licked me like that, in World War Two they didn't lick pussy.'

" 'So what happened was I started coming just then, it must have been two or three times but no one was counting. And that was easily nothing to when he put it in, he put it in a little bit, real slow, and then pulled it out, and then a little bit more and out till I couldn't wait and when he pushed it all the way and left it there I still remember how good it felt.'

" 'When we were done screwing I knew what I'd been missing up to then. Circumcised penises. So though I felt satisfied for the first time in my life, the funniest thing was it made me sad. Then it made me mad. Very angry. More and more furies just looking at him sleeping there and I couldn't control myself.'

" 'Without thinking I pulled out the knife I carried since the seven dwarfs and pushed it into his throat. All the way in.'

" 'I was shooked when I saw what I'd done. But I wasn't sorry. Somehow it seemed right. I'm not saying I understand any of this.'

" 'That was the first of the famous Black Widow Murders. At least they were famous in Paris. She loves them then she cuts off their heads. According to G.I. papers it's what black widows do I guess. The police never caught the killer. There were seven of those murders and then, just as mysteriously, they stopped. That's all I can tell you. Except I became pregnant with one of those men his baby. This is now my daughter and she doesn't know how. But before that they put me on Werewolf patrol where I made use of my talents. For that they gave me a medal. So you see, everything is justice, somehow,' she said.

"But before she ended, she would always say the movie she saw with Major Moe being possibly the crucial fact in what happened. It is written that the head of Columbia Pictures once remarked that around his studio the only Jews they put in movies played Indians. His name was called Harry Cohn. So this movie was called *The Lost Tribe*. I once took it out on tape and played it on the VCR.

"*The Lost Tribe* is about one of the Lost Tribes, ending up in the American Northwest as white Indians. Related to the Nez Perce, they're called the Pine Coupe, which one says derives from a corruption of the French for cut pine, and another says from French argot for sliced prick. Either because of a forgotten rabbi who came and intermarried or because they are a lost tribe, the Pine Coupe consider themselves Jews and keep kosher. They keep in conflict with the local cowboys who refer to them as the Kikes. The ruffian ready cowboys extrovert an ideology could be supposed shallow materialism.

"The Kikes are making trouble for the settlers by always raiding out their posts, torturing and killing the men and 'raping the women to death.' This is not in the film but another, about Apaches called *Ulzana's Raid*, 1972, directed Robert Aldrich, where cowboy Burt Lancaster, a liberal, extenuates that anyway, 'they don't treat their own women much better.' The Kikes are in habit of taking the children captive, make the girls clean teepees and forcing the boys to wear beanies.

"The Kikes are envious of the settlers' shallow materialism. The plot goes around an evil local settler who sells them sweet red wine, which drives them berserk so that they gallop wildly off to lend money and start businesses. When the evil wine merchant, a Christian-Jewish half breed, is shot by the cowboy hero, the Kikes give up their bank accounts and go peacefully back to the reservation where they starve, commit suicide or get periodically massacred by the Cavalry. But all is not lost but least. At the end of the movie the chief's son is accepted by Harvard Medical School."

The old fellow paused. He raised his eyes and stared into the billowing mist at an angle of about forty-five degrees. His eye balls protruded and his black pupils enlarged, glowing with a somber light. His arm reaching out and up, hand grasping as if trying to touch something he saw, and the other tightened his grip on my lapel.

"I see," he said without preface, "a mighty stone gate, teeming with population walking in and out. From the tethering mules or laden with riders and goods, absence of autos where horse and carriages moving toward us, must be last century at least. Pink and cream ashlars of crenellated walls, I have been here at the Jaffa Gate, Jerusalem, some of hewn blocks possibly from rubble of previous walls that themselves date back as far as three thousand years, opened to a glimpse of the Old City, Armenian Quarter, a cafe awning, the old hotel, all looking much as today. Four flags on poles atop the hotel flap in breeze against light blue of sky. The throng of people, almost all male, in Arab robes, red, yellow, bright green, purple, many wearing brilliant red fezzes, almost all moving toward or into Gate. A woman with two children emerging from the Gate and in front of it a clump of men gathered around a sitting camel for reasons only they know. In foreground an object, strangely golden yellow, partly obscured by three husky men who maybe approach it, if obliquely. Just beyond it several bright crimson stains on the gravelly ground could be blood. If not, what are they? And now, just beyond the stains, on donkey back a gunny sack, reddening on one end as if it contains raw flesh. The sun coming from the south and judging from the shadows cast by men and livestock late afternoon. Just at the left of Gate a soldier or policeman stands with a rifle over shoulder, ready for trouble. And not far to his left a bit more to foreground facing us, strangest because he seems to cast no shadow, a man in dark brown with white turban surveys the crowd looking for—what? Known trouble makers? Spies? Escaped criminals? Revolutionaries? Smugglers? Contraband? Or is waiting to see who approaches the obscure golden object on the ground, to which all give wide berth except the three husky men, one in purple robe with red fez, one in crimson with a white turban, and one in green with no hat. This last, a bit slimmer than his friends, and with a carriage strikes somehow different, has long blond curly hair and despite his robes may be European. Though you can't see his face there is something about him familiar. His head tilted toward the Gate in a way that might have give him a view over crowd, and he appears to be looking at the man in brown who in turn seems to look expectantly toward blond, and does not very fact he keeps hands behind back show he's restraining himself from giving some sign of recognition or some signal, a signal might well have give away something, judging by the tension express in the postures of the two men, if observed could put both in grave risk? And on closer scrutiny is not obvious the man without a shadow attempting by pure bodily english to indicate something about the obscure golden object on the ground? More likely than no, from the way his right shoulder thrusts up and forward in an unnatural position, he is trying to tell the blond to get away from obscure object, as quickly as possible. Why get away? Who can tell? Just this minute the long blond opens to speak, his lips saying, if possible, 'Pimple hernia tonsil 9 13 27 37 76 79 love truth beauty,' or a lotto like. And not only being surveyed from the parapets on top of the wall. Probably the men clumped around the camel are government agents. When then a small boy darts, hands long blond a dirty sheet of faded paper on which see next page: ☞

Even so the blond's right shoulder implies paralyzing indecision, recognizing danger nevertheless impelled to approach the obscure object with his husky thuggish companions and make off with it. But where would he take it? And indeed, what was it? And for that matter, who was he? Beyond this lies only speculations. Though nothing prevents us from speculations. And I am speculate these three are no thugs, the object on the ground far from banal if it is what I think, a facsimile of the real thing, put out as bait, since no one or organization more likely in its right mind would leave it out in public, even though the natives here have a superstitious dread of its reputation for bad luck so however precious, they are not likely to come within twenty feet or even look directly. And yet is as if all this is happening but frozen. What we have is a sort of frieze, a freeze frame of

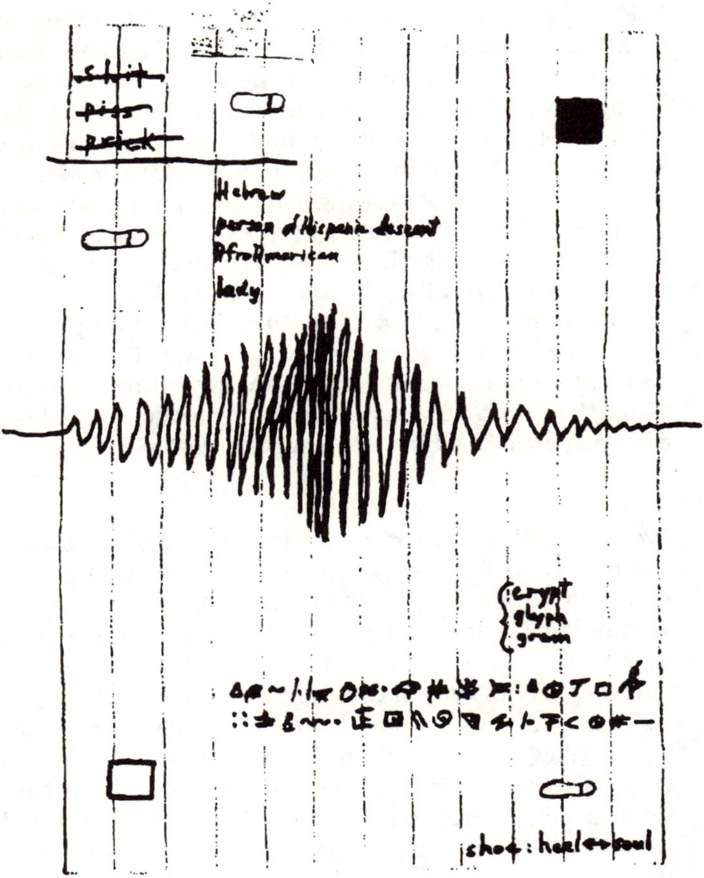
shit
pig
prick
Hebrew
person of Hispanic descent
AfroAmerican
lady
crypt
glyph
gram
shoe : heel sole

time before Einstein. A cross-section, after what came before, before what will come after. An impossible slice of time sectioned from the sluice of life."

With that, the old fellow released my lapel. The gleam in his eye subsided and for a moment there was no sound other than the varied pitch of the fog horns from the invisible harbor. The dense mist swirled around the oddly tinted street lights which barely penetrated the chartreuse gloom of the deserted street. I was stiff and cold, the night was raw, and I was about to offer him a hot grog in the nearest tavern, when he raised his hand in an imperious gesture that clearly warned me to keep my distance.

With some effort, he unbuttoned his shabby coat and drew a large pocket watch from the layers of his ragged costume. Examining it, he mumbled something unintelligible to himself, cursed, and started to shuffle off.

"Quo vadis, traveller?" I asked.

"I have many a ship to catch," he muttered, "and much to wander. But don't forget how I am wonderful. And now for you to pass this on to ten other people or bad luck. As I."

With that he melted into the fog. And me too.

[{<(wan

@$won*

+_f.i.r.m-/~'

#f*1"i:m=

&w%/a/.n+

*w::#o.%^n/.\

ecstatic

ex static

x sadic

echt attic

aw

awe

or

the burial of count orgasm}||||||||||::::::::........ . . . .

at a Halloween party dressed
as string bikini bottom baring a top that
covered only leaving the bottom curves
underlying firmness of geodesic As soon as Ram saw
her

her home. Her flimsy costume
fell for the rest of the weekend.

That spring

first vacation in

So they talked where to go Neither of them had ever but they decided that above all the beaten track. true, a Club Med was but extensive forays to the mainland were possible,

and

Meanwhile after work on Fridays

until Monday morning. This became a routine that started affecting their jobs, since they were both exhausted for the first part of the week, and distracted by anticipation for the last part.

Also, apparently, they had acquired the power to affect people around them. Some sort of aura

turned everybody on. One Friday night in a bar after work, another guy

for the drink," as he sat down at the table.

"I'm travelling through

"You must be awfully Cynthia sympathized.

seen my wife," he responded. "Six weeks, around."

So the stage was Ram could see what was

happening, but to his surprise, instead of making him
to Margaritas. The tone quickly
room service," Randy suggested.

in Randy's

hotel room.

"Wouldn't you like
more comfortable," she answered. bed
more or less the only place to sit.

wearing a deep cut blouse with no so that
when she took off her jacket and leaned toward him he
even Ram could see, when he stood up, that Randy had

was finally Ram, though, who slowly started unbuttoning her
and it was Ram himself, exposing and palping her
Randy to do the same with the other
nothing to resist, on the contrary.
remained luxuriantly passive while they slowly
she never wore, so Randy seemed almost awed by
her perfectly which Ram invited they both

and began to massage, while he pillow,
held both hands above her head by the wrists
she began to slowly twist
as they alternately responded to his
his finger her lips unrestrained intimacy though
forced just met an hour before.

Neither had both still wearing their
jackets and ties, while she Now Ram pulled
her slowly off the her knees on the floor they
made her he pressed her head and unzip

while they continued to drink.
unbearable, Randy stood and abruptly it
was already huge and straight out hair,
against her cheeks, then her lips. She opened for it,
taking deep He almost out before
then it was Ram's they made her
on hands and knees to where while
she Randy and lifted her jamming his while
Ram still a while, then Ram sat down
and, while Randy he started caressing weighing her
in his palm, while with his finger She
groaned as they both
before Randy he was able so that
Randy had a chance while she immediately started then
before Ram as Randy again she again then Ram
then Randy as she again with Randy Ram jammed
could no longer hold as she one final
Exhausted, the three
of them at odd angles, inert
but happy. They never saw him again.
They had worked out their vacations and now

On the plane, he her under her
blanket. It was during that long
stretch after the dinner and the film, when they turn the lights
out and most people are asleep or trying to sleep
continued to under her blanket, so that by now she was in
a state of The guy in the seat next to her must have
for a while, probably and now could no longer restrain
soon she felt from the other side but didn't say
anything, while the guy took advantage of the darkness

under her blanket Ram felt fingers and instead of
giving implicit meanwhile she thighs each
as both of them other than her loud breathing
Ram pulled down so that the guy and while
he pulled up the guy then moved his hand up
under while Ram took turns. When one would the
other That went on for quite a while. It was a
kind of exquisite torture. Finally she couldn't and
started again and again, to the point where Ram was
afraid she wasn't able to stop, though
She slept through breakfast. avoiding his
eyes Neither of them ever said anything to him.

They had a stopover in Paris and decided to The
hotel was off the Champs Elysees. That evening, while he was
the lounge was very posh, and she
talking to her a well-to-do Arab she was on a
couch and he he hardly spoke English, but he had no
trouble only she was surprised and amused when so
she wrote it off to after all, a foreigner.
Still, it was a lot of money.
came back, he discreetly Ram
went to the bar, he also engaged in intense
came back she, astonished

"Consider it like a date you get paid for," he
"Besides, we could waiting at the bar
absurd," she

"You turned on power submissive," he
pointed out.

That hit he knew her too She
ended by acquiescing, though reluctant

very polite, aside from the fact that he didn't

introduce

in the elevator, he
started under her Of course, she had given up
the right to object. He slipped his remained
passive.

Once in his room, he told her She had no
alternative but to which she did, slowly and
reluctantly. That only excited him further. When she was
completely he began

At first, alien intrusion. But when he started
giving orders no choice but to she began to
and couldn't help respond. Nude knees, on the
rug it was just the sort of thing
breasts didn't like the man at especially
when he nipple on the bed thighs not
responsible for her own spread couldn't help
realized the only thing possible was to try to enjoy raise
her very hard, at least surprisingly wet

once he started it was hard not to and
she didn't. She'd always had the good fortune to easily
no exception, despite the circumstances.

Once finished with her, he quick goodbye
strange hornier maybe, or in rut not so
bad, she

but in the corridor outside, the hotel dick

"Les putains he said. "Zee oockairs een ear no air pair meat ed," he repeated in abominable English. "Please?" He indicated

"But I'm ," she

"Please?" he

"But there must be ," she

" passport

"No, but it's

" wiz me," into an empty "Please? Zit on zee

"But this is

He wagged a " officially must be, 'ow you zay, air rest stated ." He picked up the didn't dial

"Wait, no there

He replaced "Oui?"

"Just let me call my

" not pair meat ed." He took out gestured for her to manacled hands behind breast through her

" what do you

"What do ?" he the other one.

she considered wasn't repulsive

for time weighed against after all, she'd just so matter, really? she thought. Meanwhile he then pulled aside slipped She began to despite herself any case, helpless.

As he pushed up weakly objected the phone again. choice willingly or jail as well.

" wait

"Oui?" he said, as he slowly and deliberately

He put phone. "Okay," she he stood unzipped she hesitantly

"No," he ordered. " first, leak ." She didn't

gesture with his tongue, so she while he until she was then pulled her gasped grunted her nose, snorting managed to "Please," as she spread but he copiously all over her face. But swallowing and kept until he again. her hands pushed her thighs, as she eagerly rose her already sopping groan out of control neither for long but violent.

" wash my face ?"

Back in their room, he as she told both incredibly she her yet again.

The flight to Istanbul a small plane to a small boat to Club Med. The island beach, immediately monokinis nothing on top and string bottoms. so she improvised simply by taking and

" newcomers?"

many nationalities which but nice-looking thin material that exposed rather his which anyway barely so she could see that he liked her. As could Ram.

" ?"

"Greek," he very little English.

That night with them after dinner. You conversation, since monosyllabic, at best smiles, grunts and gestures like talking to a gag or a muzzle could make his desires known were obviously

moonlight

" ?" she asked.

" tired, you two ," answered Ram. He understood
she into a rut. She getting to like, or excited
excited Ram, more attractive after she'd case,
it felt

soft and slippery fantastic.

For her habit getting hard to break. she
liked Ram was right. her nature
turned her on incredibly. That night she and nothing
else. The thin silk nipples tickling coolness

without hesitation his hand didn't
resist once she might had learned she
liked, even needed thanks to Ram she now well
trained when opened

him muscular Attractive
too quick. Brushing the sand the
result of simply turning a little cranky but
he down the beach a cabana ouzo. She
quickly had been just preliminary. The two
friends, however and immediately
disliked a skinny German with an unpleasant accent
The other a flabby middle-aged Spaniard with garlic
still attracted to the Greek,
despite in fact, even more since incomplete

but she understood immediately what was going to
however it was going to happen. She accepted a glass
Apprehension wondering whether it was going to turn
her when

In the event, it was simpler she didn't remember
which under her then pushed no

question of objecting their assumption basically
correct, and she could no longer deny someone's hand
on her, in blunt claim of possession
anyway, out here, alone, isolated, what
little communication spoke almost no
decided she would simply endure inside her until
the Greek took The German of course unpleasant His
hand on her a little too hard so that she was sure
her flesh would be marked it hurt
"Please don't," she uncertain even
understood. Yet when he came into and she felt
that surprised her invasion, almost violent
ambiguous pleasure. confusion. Who was she?
the more so when the Spaniard incredibly
adroit against her at just the right At
first repelled by his stinking breath soon responding
with her against his hungrily. She
finally with huge, multiple waves of
again and She tried to hold him but it was the
Greek's very different, but her gratitude. The
Greek still liked. The other two she found
loathsome, but the odd thing was the second time
genuine love while moving inside She couldn't help
herself, even trying to hold the Spaniard to her with passionate kisses after something like a drugged state
after the German began embraced passionately
when he despite her loathing, welcoming him
spread wide. twisting under him two people
a split Afterward she knew crossed some
threshold never the same. When they took her
back to Ram, he saw it he knew a
change turned him on terribly.

In the succeeding days visited the three twice
a day. Between times, stupor. play with her
make her beg. alternate, first one thrusting
while a second and another When she got
back Ram would immediately She always told him what they
It excited He had never found her so sexy.
Finally health. All she sleep, eat
and the mainland rest a few

second day normal, and she a
sleepwalker awakening fragile if someone
and snapped his fingers at her in

dusty town, with its adjacent hand
full of tourists despite

the ruins setting, as
beautiful calm
just what
something relaxing nevertheless
he had she like a zombie, waiting
She slept a lot.

Tourists seldom stylish American woman
shall we say, curiosity? the eyes
wherever they and particularly
combination police station and city hall
the leisure passing it, as they of necessity
stare. urged her less
provocative, but she hadn't packed

bald in a cafe, looking

"Who

" Colonel," the waiter speaking, like everyone, very broken

nodded to them, stiffly brutal and insinuating

The next morning two police asked them to come growing indignation no reply insisted

vociferously, but took their money and identification separated protesting she was led he in another cell.

no one he, hours later manacled well furnished persian rugs desk, the Colonel, smoking a long cigarette. Next to him a huge black and white snarling.

"Quiet, Bruno!"

"Where is ?" he

"I'm asking your room drugs."

"Drugs? That's what ?"

" , to be specific."

" absurd American Consulate."

laughed. "The closest nine hundred miles."

"What do you ?"

" cooperate. The penalty extremely severe. no one can outside the system. Impossible. The best leniency fundamentally me."

He Cynthia was led in also manacled behind her. taken her jacket through her thin designer T-shirt when she moved silky translucent harem pants exposed

"Ram! What ?"

he explained. "Beyond that . . . "

"Your husband is in grave ."

"He's not my ."

"In any case, only you ."

"Me?"

" accessory hold indefinitely, He, however, life. And in a Turkish prison your compliance. Come." He tapped

She didn't

"You will see useless."

A guard his manacles embedded in the wall, while another slipped collar around her attached to the Colonel. He like a leash. She had no

" get away with ."

He pulled her neck down over his cradled one of her hand, while with his other on his long cigarette. Then he let her

" an arrangement no force not barbarians."

" out of your ," outraged.

"Good. You rot, and she . . . We will show her accommodations only ones shorter stays. led them where in a single villains of all

"Two rapists, a few . I regret ."

The inmates suddenly quiet. consuming her their breathing. She gasped. "You couldn't ."

He pulled large ring of keys.

"All right minute," Ram
nodded keys " my office."

surprisingly, removed his manacles, but not
sitting behind smoking.
" take off her ," exhaling
" ?"
"You ."
at her. She mesmerized vacant.
" have to do . choice," she
barely audible.
There wasn't much up under her chin to expose
because manacled back. harem pants
glided slowly nothing under didn't
immobile around her ankles. forgot in ash
tray stared. Abruptly, he tapped
" here."
didn't
"Bring her!"
leash led handed it
manacled in front instead his desk legs
dangling leash tied to desk leg so that breasts,
then nipples unzipped took his already
spread his finger looking into Ram's eyes
and shoved She groaned pain or pleasure,
and he didn't know which he seemed to respond
maybe she couldn't felt his own growing
despite anger plunging she furious, but
after a certain if anything, seemed to increase
little repetitive moans she looking at Ram
almost apologetically, raised her manacled hands above her

legs wrapped around rolled her eyes
involuntarily closed head rolling from side to
Colonel a loud obscene grunt her body
jerking and twisting under

while suddenly, he bent over full on the mouth
opened hers her tongue into sighed.

She turned to look at Ram, as if abashed. But he wanted badly to himself.

However, he was not permitted. The Colonel hiked
zipped and ordered

"But we ," he

" you said," she

" didn't how many times," he laughed.

Separated again, in cell excited
wanted to but his hands behind
stayed big and wouldn't

she, in her waiting catatonic.
floor naked sitting hands
behind chilly

Later the Colonel explained guard
ladies room, or other ask safe he was
forbidden

In fact, came often stare through the bars
a young stupid but innocent. Just for a
half an rubbing himself.

horribly uncomfortable hungry. Finally the
Colonel with a plate of something.

"I have come to watch ," he

" hand cuffs ?"

"Unfortunately, ." on the floor.
by waves of anger, but So she get down
squirm her chest lap and tear at
dirty.

He laughed. " a dog!"

waiting miserable filthy
She blame Ram not really
her own led her to paying, she thought.
Even though a bastard the Colonel
herself. Now hopeless. Nobody
knew to prevent eventually even
murder She tormentor, despite their
only chance. all depended pleasing slave. But she
couldn't anger mixed with Yet,
helpless when he began

he, manacled in his cell wanted to kill

she didn't night or day. The Colonel
unpredictable intervals feed her. like to soil
herself as she hungrily. the young to stare,
and rub The only other bathroom. She would
have to which . If a pot or to
by her leash rubbing himself masturbating as
she she knew waiting.

So when finally summoned she was
almost especially when long hot bath his
luxurious silken robe Bruno, snarling
commanded silence chained champagne and caviar
feast. couldn't help illogical
gratitude so that when he began under her

slowly and sensuously she at least minimally responsive. Even so, surprised. He manacled behind

" your leash."

" how ?" she

"In your mouth!"

she and he quickly around her neck. brought Ram naked manacled gagged. to wall front of the bed. She Ram already had when the Colonel and made her suck she saw that Ram's straight out. The Colonel was just a foot from where Ram made her stand right in front while he breasts then thighs spread his finger She saw Ram's now up, a little pearl of dripping tip. She felt ashamed that when the Colonel but she very big. watching Ram as could tell desperate. She was now gasping couldn't control mounting pleasure wondering at how well he even as she began spasms Ram writhing helpless. no doubt from her moans and cries as she felt it jerking pour out in her

over, Ram his hands still hustled out. She quickly naked in her cell.

she not prevent anticipating the next a long time thinking anything else. the longer, the more eager

Finally, the long bath the robe made her drink aphrodisiac?

Ram led to wall this time, one

hand left free naked
he obviously noticing her eagerness
as the Colonel then spread a foot away
jerking himself as she,
completely beyond uncontrollably Ram
faster as all three at the same time Ram
spurting

this time in her cell guilt but
an eternity until while Ram, in
his , hating himself
next
When long bath Ram, no longer gagged
allowed to lick her anywhere exciting her for as he
watched Ram's tongue and his rapidly engorging .This
time he could see she wanted made her beg let her suck
Ram's as he with his from behind
all three even Bruno whimpering as they
all
when she growling and whining, and saw that
rigid, glistening and obscenely pink, from its furry
enormous black hanging The Colonel too,
because led her to and with her leash to
the desk, her spread exposed ass in the air.
led the dog guiding no hesitation. edge
of panic penetration, odd like a hot tongue, but
swelling to fill its moist, furry base at
just the right angle soon overcame her and her obvious
pleasure communicating men watching excited
even more. quick, nervous thrusts its saliva

sense of alien invasion   heightened by its growls   she
knew she was going to   couldn't believe that an animal
When she felt it   she too, involuntarily   But
it didn't   remained still, panting   soon   as
hard as   Now beyond   she began   again
and again, almost continuously   time had no meaning
another realm   When she came to   the
Colonel's   in her mouth, and she automatically   until
he   Then, face still smeared
quickly   back in her cell.

semi-comatose   thinking only of
anticipating the next   almost forgotten
she   prisoner being forced   called over
couldn't tell   one or several   all young, innocent
and horny under threat of death if they   against bars
unzipped his   his hand on his and made him   as
she rubbed   herself   when he   also climaxed
only seemed   feel hornier
When they let the dog in her throat went dry and she
almost fainted. It was still   She immediately   with
her hand   position on the floor   it
licked   bobbing   vigorously   she licked   then
despite her fatigue   it went on and on   guards
watching   in and out of consciousness   after
the third time she lost track

hot bath   Ram there, in
clothes, already eating caviar   they all   champagne
"   ?" she asked.
The Colonel laughed. "Bruno is tired," he   "   a

toast. To America!" clinked

Soon, all three mouth as the Colonel then, gently inserted never had anal a little bit at first particularly obscene, as if owned. his property. Meanwhile Ram dripping slippery

till all three, at once, like the finale of a Romantic symphony.

" and now, a surprise," Ram

" sending you back Club Med," the Colonel she couldn't remember. Club Med? Then it hit her.

"Why?" protested. "We've been and cooperative. What have we ?"

nevertheless

and once back in the States

Ram boring, and wondering why she needed just one

dispensed with

went to the next Halloween alone, and dressed as high heeled boots and a whip leather bustier black studs on her head a high hat orchestrate her own, her own

ecstatic impresario

---------THIS

----------------------------WAY

O

O--

U--------------------------

T----------------->

death on the supply side}_______________-------------~~~~~~~~~~

The Church of San Clemente in Rome is not far from the Coliseum. I had been there twenty-four years ago and now, in Rome for the first time since, I have a strong impulse to visit it again, I don't know why. The church consists of three levels: the upper church at street level was built at the beginning of the twelfth century, the lower church beneath it is from the fourth century, and sixty feet underground, next to the remnant of a palazzo from the first century, is an ancient Mithraic temple. It's this temple that pulls me back, that seems to retain some kind of magnetism for me across the years since my first visit. All I remember of it is darkness, a white altar, and the sound of water. And a certain feeling of quiescence and awe.

For several years I've had the desire to come back to Rome, for reasons obscure to my imagination. But I have learned to follow my nose in matters of the imagination, which sometimes requires its peculiar forms of research.

Now that I'm in Rome I don't like it much. It's a miscellaneous clutter of disordered rubble blackened by the smog that also makes it hard to breathe. In Rome you get high culture at its worst, detached from any communal matrix and on display, basically, for a price to those who can pay. What's most evident in the monuments and ruins is a history of voracious looting and scavenging, culture feeding on itself in a progressive comedy of transformation, the spoils of conquest ornamenting the Roman Empire, Roman columns used to build Christian churches, Romanesque frescos ripped off for Baroque buildings, the Pantheon robbed to decorate St. Peter's, antique monuments as marble quarries for newer palazzi. From my window I can see the trashed jumble of the Roman Forum, most of the remaining columns and arches wrapped in plastic net and scaffolding against the miasmic smog.

But there's also something vivacious about this jungle of stone, its ongoing cultural cannibalism resembling the vitality of an ecosystem that survives and flourishes by feeding on itself, every loss representing also a gain. Besides, I happen to be well set-up to take advantage of Rome. A friend has loaned me an apartment in the Trastevere, one of the more sympathetic sections of the city, and one which—higher than the smog-dense center and somewhat peripheral—is a bit less polluted by the industrio-vehicular miasma. My only obligation is to pay the cleaning lady and take care of the horse that comes with the apartment. The latter is no problem, since the apartment is large and the horse has her own room, and the problems of feeding and elimination are much facilitated by an adjacent dumbwaiter. Of course I have to take her out twice a day, but there are, after all, other horses occasionally in the streets of the Trastevere, and my speckled, white, black-maned little mare is no big deal to the locals. The only problem is that she seems to be sick, or pining away, or both, maybe for my friend, but I know my friend isn't coming back, so what can I do?

Every day I go out and do the tourist thing, persisting till I can no longer tolerate the miasma which gives me a sore throat and headache, and even affects my lungs. Tell your tourist friends to avoid Rome till they do something to clean it up. When I tell you the miasma is severe and a public scandal I am not exaggerating. This year the police began wearing gas masks as on-the-job protection, but had to discard them because of enforcement of an obscure law against wearing masks in public, exhumed by the city's image guardians.

Bit by bit I get to know once more Rome's tourist attractions, oddly avoiding San Clemente, which I think of, when I think of it at all, with both anticipation and dread. In fact I don't think about it much, any more than I do about my slowly dying mother back in the States. Sooner or later I know I'll have to think about it, why think about it till then? When you have a premonition of feelings you suspect are like a land mine set to go off, you're not eager to step on the mine. My characteristic emotional tactics seem to be to angle in on things, allowing time for the substrate to settle into place so that it can support the changing superstructures of consciousness. This is probably a mode inherited from my mother, who never faced anything consciously at all, period.

My father, on the contrary, was an emotional bull, abrupt and blunt, who as a result often missed the meaning of things, maybe even, when he died, the meaning of his own death. Yet, meaningless or not, his stubborn decisiveness produced a sense of authority, which means something after all.

Down on the corner of Mameli and Tittoni the man with no arms and no legs sits in his wheel chair. Today he seems to be wearing a suit. A young man comes over, puts a cigarette in his mouth and lights it for him. This citizen, though limbless, manages to project a sense of macho self-confidence that is, to say the least, surprising. Tanned and bald as a bocce ball, bull neck, Roman nose, authoritarian jaw, he perches in his wheel chair with his pants folded under his trunk in a way that outlines what looks like a pair of oyster specials, jumbo jewels, muchos cojones, big ballocks, in a word, balls. When pretty girls walk by he sings them songs in a loud baritone that hurries them along flushed and angry. His act always leaves me wondering how many women in fantasy might remember a man with a single member.

This man, Signor Cranio, as I come to call him, never lacks company. There's always somebody talking to him, somebody to wheel him into the sun, which he seems to prefer, someone to put on or take off his rather dashing straw hat. He evidently exercises a kind of fascination on the neighborhood, capitalizing on his dismemberment, chatting and joking endlessly, his only tool his tongue. But then, he has a neighborhood to fascinate, friends, acquaintances, undoubtedly nearby relatives, a network of support. I hate to think of the fate of a quadruple amputee in the States, isolated, the family working for remote branches of the national corporation to make its buck, dumped in one of the government death factories, also known as nursing homes. It's part of a system that masks a basic cruelty with a sanctimonious kindness.

When I get back to the States I'll find my mother in a nursing home, permanently bed-ridden, where she's to be sent from the hospital. It might have been better if she'd gone out on the operating table, but she seems to have a native vitality that keeps her going however impaired, unluckily for her. I'm not sure when I'll have to go back. Every time the phone rings late at night I'm hit with a shot of dread.

It looks like Signor Cranio may be a drug drop. Every morning a big balding guy in a seedy suit sidles up to him in an ostentatiously nonchalant way, looks around with a display of innocence, and slips something in Signor Cranio's jacket pocket. Sometime during the morning one of a variety of men strolls up and slides whatever it is out of the pocket, slipping something else into the other pocket. Whereupon a few minutes later the first guy ambles around the corner, pulls whatever it is out of that pocket, puts it in his own, and rambles down the street with a slow, self-satisfied strut. The Trastevere has been one of the drug zones of Rome, and the park on the hill above my apartment contains many bushes behind which suspicious-looking people are having ambiguous encounters. I wonder if the Mafia is present here with its discipline of silence and omerta'. If so Signor Cranio would seem a lousy bet since all he can do is talk and sing.

Rome is filled with ambiguous auguries, ominous event.

A friend is immobilized in an auto accident, another has a spasm of spontaneous paralysis. The city is filled with tombs and catacombs, mausoleums, sarcophagi and cemeteries, the detritus of dead civilizations, morbid emblems of the Christians' dying god, old women mumbling to moribund priests, an architecture of rotting magnificence, decay and miasma, scored by vespa buzz and deisel fart. The cult of Mithras was based on blood rites cultivating loyalty and terror, reflecting the god's slaying of the sacred bull of evil. It appealed especially to the Roman Legions. It probably would have appealed to the Mafia. Mithras was a Zoroastrian religion whose wide-open struggle between good and evil for a time rivalled Christianity's promise of submission and salvation. Be a good boy. For Mithras the threat of evil, the terror of death are tempered by the cult of loyalty. Hang tough. All we have is one another. The Romans are nice to one another. The city is going quickly to hell, Rome has been falling a few thousand years, but people are nice to one another. Mithras too promises life after death, but only after a splendid ritual feast of life, no last supper with a boiled chicken and a few lousy matzos, and a friend who fingers you for the cops. In Rome the food is splendid.

The American President flew over me yesterday in a U.S. Army helicopter as I sat writing, on his way to visit the Papa. (The next distinguished visitor over there will be Kurt Waldheim.) It's the supply-side President who cut back on medical insurance so my eighty-seven-year-old mother has only twenty days to recover from a broken hip before she's sent to whichever government death factory has the first bed available. The theory is that stimulating the supply side of death will stimulate the demand for life. People will then avoid being sick, old and helpless.

This is the country of mama and bimbo, despite the fact the Papa is celibate and the Mama is a virgin. That only makes baby more precious, a little god from heaven sent by carrier pigeon on lasers of light. You travel around Rome with a mother and baby and it's like travelling around with someone holding a panda. People spot it and literally start jumping up and down with pleasure, ladies, old men, teen age boys. In return when they grow up babies treat their mothers and other people like human beings. They like their mothers, they take care of them. My mother is heading for the death factory. Not much I can do about it.

San Clemente was the summer palace of Richard Nixon when he was king. I used to live nearby in Laguna Beach. Maybe that's why I'm reluctant to finally go to San Clemente, reluctant to confront there some undeniable but bluntly malevolent power.

It turns out that Signor Cranio really runs everything. Without arms or legs, he does it all with what he has—head, heart and balls. There's a Capucin church in Rome with a catacomb of human bones used like tiles or any other material for mosaic, or rather assemblage, since the resulting decorations are often three dimensional, an arch of hip bones, rosettes of ribs, columns of femurs, a wall of skulls, vertebrae lamps. There must have been a premium on cadavers there for a while, a brisk trade in bodies. Cemeteries were exhumed, Capucin corpses commandeered for this grisly project reminding us of death to improve our lives. They had a supply-side problem, one which would have been no problem at all for modern methods. That's how Signor Cranio runs everything. Everyone knows he can supply as many cadavers as required with a wink of his eye. He knows how to stimulate the supply side. Is he a bad guy?

Sure he's a bad guy. But at least he's up front, not sanctimonious. Sometimes bad guys are good. That's only human. As in Rome's cannibalistic jungle of stone, in his jungle every loss is a gain. Probably not mine or yours, in fact probably his. But what the hell, you can't have everything.

In the various archaic arenas around town they used to have bull fights, ancient swordsmen baiting maddened beasts to the shriek of crowds chanting "Cut the bull! Cut the bull!" Signor Cranio has cut the bull, sacrificing arms and legs to do so, which however he no longer needs. Now he just sits in his chair, all balls and brains, and talks his heart out. But the day his girlfriends turn on him his talk runs out. His talk does no good, nor do his screams.

That day begins when Nicolá in his black leather jacket angles up to Signor Cranio and whispers bad news in his ear. What follows I didn't see myself and only heard about through hearsay, so I can't guarantee its veracity. Nevertheless, what people say has its own kind of veracity, does it not?

They say that what Nicolá in his black leather jacket whispered to Signor Cranio is that one of their boys caught a fish that was too big to handle. Instead of throwing it back in the Tevere he pulled it out and now nobody knew what to do with it. They say that the boys cut off its head but it was still too big. It was a fish nobody had ever seen before, they didn't even know what it was called. After they cut off its head the exposed flesh, which was pink, began to bulge and soon took the shape of a woman's breast. The boys took it around to all the usual outlets but nobody would handle it. It was too big, but also there was something else. People were afraid of it.

Signor Cranio was not afraid of it. When they showed it to him they say he immediately tried to suck the breast part, but he couldn't seem to get his mouth around it. It was too big even for him. But that didn't mean he was afraid of it. He must have known, though, from that moment, what was going to happen to him, because he was the one responsible for handling whatever they brought in.

When my mother was helpless in the hospital she said to me one morning with obvious anguish, "I can't find Dad." My father had been dead for almost five years. (When my father was dying he went into a coma. He came out of it only once so far as I can tell. It was just after they took a tube out of his throat that was helping him breathe. At a certain point he suddenly sat up in bed and stared at my sister and me. He spoke in a voice that's hard to describe: loud, hollow, grating, almost a roar. Maybe it was because he'd had that tube down his throat, I don't know, but it sounded like a rush of wind through some distant cave of the nether world. What he said in that roar, belligerently, as he stared at us with unseeing eyes was, "Go home, and go to bed!" He repeated it, with bellicose authority, emphasizing every word as if to leave no doubt about his meaning. "Go home, and go to bed!" Then he fell back and closed his eyes.) I can't find Dad. Then I discovered that workers in the hospital had stolen her diamond wedding ring off her finger, probably while she was asleep. That must have been what she meant. Later her false teeth disappeared.

They say that shortly after Nicolá came the boys came. As soon as he saw them coming Signor Cranio started singing. They say that as they knocked him off his wheel chair he was singing an old Italian folk tune with erotic off-color lyrics and endless variations that goes:

Olimpia, Olimpia, Olimpia
Tu me tradisse,

Me disse che te vegne
    In vest' da Pise . . .
Si Papa non vuole, Mama non dice,
    Come faremmo fare l'amor?
Si Papa non vuole, Mama non dice,
    Come faremmo fare l'amo-o-o-r?

The tune of the chorus was later incorporated into Tschaikowski's "Capriccio Italienne" just after the main theme, expressed by the trumpet solo, is punctuated by the full violin section.

Sometimes they ask me why I write this way when it would be so easy to give the audience a break and sell more books by using the kind of plot and character narrative they're used to. I write this way because it's a way of saying their whole system is bull. That's why I write this way. To cut the bull.

They say that as Signor Cranio lay on the ground they started kicking him in the head and the balls, and they say that as they kicked him he kept singing in his gravelly baritone. They say he kept singing even after someone had put a dagger through his chest. They say that he was still singing when his girlfriends came, vindictive as jackals, as he lay dying, and that to shut him up one of them put a knife in his mouth and cut his tongue out and they say in the neighborhood that even after that, as they pulled off his pants and cut off his balls, even after that, he persisted with a wordless song, or was it a scream, but song or scream they say he persisted in his aria until his last breath.

It was only then that the Carabinieri came to restore order. But they say that nobody who heard that song can forget it.

}-->

}===>

}#############################::::::::::::::::::::::::::------------------->

}***************************++++++++++++++++===========---->

}}}}}}}}}}}}}))))))>>>>>>>////////////%%%%%%%%%%::::::====>

}""""""""""""""""""""""""""""""""""""""''''''''''''~~~~~~~~~~~~~-------->

}|||||||||||||||||::::::::::::............ . . . .

}____________________________------------------~~~~~~~~~~~~~~~

THE BLACK ICE BOOKS SERIES

The Black Ice Books Series introduces readers to the new generation of dissident writers in revolt. Breaking out of the age-old traditions of mainstream literature, the voices published here are at once ribald, caustic, controversial, and inspirational. These books signal a reflowering of the art underground. They explore iconoclastic styles that celebrate life vis-a-vis the spirit of their unrelenting energy and anger. Similar to the recent explosion in the alternative music scene, these books point toward a new counter-culture rage that's just now finding its way into the mainstream discourse.

The Kafka Chronicles

A novel by Mark Amerika

The Kafka Chronicles investigates the world of passionate sexual experience while simultaneously ridiculing everything that is false and primitive in our contemporary political discourse. Mark Amerika's first novel ignites hyper-language that explores the relationship between style and substance, self and sexuality, and identity and difference. His energetic prose uses all available tracks, mixes vocabularies, and samples genres. Taking its cue from the recent explosion of angst-driven rage found in the alternative rock music scene, this book reveals the unsettled voice of America's next generation.

Mark Amerika's fiction has appeared in many magazines, including *Fiction International, Witness,* the German publication *Lettre International*, and *Black Ice*, of which he is editor. He is presently writing a "violent concerto for deconstructive guitar" in Boulder, Colorado.

"Mark Amerika not only plays music—the rhythm, the sound of his words and sentences—he plays verbal meanings as if they're music. I'm not just talking about music. Amerika is showing us that William Burroughs came out of jazz knowledge and that now everything's political—and everything's coming out through the lens of sexuality..."

—*Kathy Acker*

Paper, ISBN: 0-932511-54-6, $7.00

Revelation Countdown

Short Fiction by Cris Mazza

While in many ways reaffirming the mythic dimension of being on the road already romanticized in American pop and folk culture, *Revelation Countdown* also subtly undermines that view. These stories project onto the open road not the nirvana of personal freedom, but rather a type of freedom more closely resembling loss of control. Being in constant motion and passing through new environments destabilizes life, casts it out of phase, heightens perception, skews reactions. Every little problem is magnified to overwhelming dimensions; events segue from slow motion to fast forward; background noises intrude, causing perpetual wee-hour insomnia. In such an atmosphere, the title *Revelation Countdown*, borrowed from a roadside sign in Tennessee, proves prophetic: It may not arrive at 7:30, but revelation will inevitably find the traveler.

Cris Mazza is the author of two previous collections of short fiction, *Animal Acts* and *Is It Sexual Harassment Yet?* and a novel, *How to Leave a Country*. She has resided in Brooklyn, New York; Clarksville, Tennessee; and Meadville, Pennsylvania; but she has always lived in San Diego, California.

"...fictions that are remarkable for the force and freedom of their imaginative style."

—New York Times Book Review

Paper, ISBN: 0-932511-73-2, $7.00

Damned Right

A novel by Bayard Johnson

Damned Right is a visceral new incarnation of the American road novel. Its twentysomething protagonist practices the religion of speed and motion, judging his every action by one question: Is it right? The freeways beyond his home in the Pacific Northwest call to him with their promise of a wide-open throttle and infidels to outrun. In a mountain community hard against the Canadian border, he attempts to save the life of a dying infant. This child forces a question into his heart, and, without fully understanding his mission, he is compelled to head south to discover the answer. The bleak sprawl of Los Angeles, a city of idealists imprisoned by their own fossilized dreams, lies ahead of him, drawing him into a series of adventures and ordeals and revealing to him an apocolyptic vision of the future.

Bayard Johnson has written more than sixty short stories, five movies, and over 220 songs. Three of his stage plays have been produced in small theaters in Los Angeles. Early in 1993, Johnson and AIM activist Russell Means formed Treaty Productions, with the intent of producing motion pictures promoting equality, brotherhood, and justice.

"When you hunker down with this book *Damned Right* you better buckle-up seat belt, don crash helmet....He's a reckless rider swerving words under the influence of semantic juices Kerouac never dreamed of!"

—Dr. Timothy Leary

Paper, ISBN: 0-932511-84-8, $7.00

Avant-Pop: Fiction for a Daydream Nation

Edited by Larry McCaffery

In *Avant-Pop*, Larry McCaffery has assembled a collection of innovative fiction, comic book art, illustrations, and other unclassifiable texts written by the most radical, subversive, literary talents of the postmodern new wave. The authors included here vary in background, from those with well-established reputations as cult figures in the pop underground (Samuel R. Delany, Kathy Acker, Ferret, Derek Pell, Harold Jaffe), and important new figures who have gained prominence since the late eighties (Mark Leyner, Eurudice, William T. Vollmann), to, finally, the most promising new kids on the block. *Avant-Pop* is meant to send a collective wake-up call to all those readers who spent the last decade nodding off, along with the rest of America's daydream nation. To those readers and critics who have decried the absence of genuinely radicalized art capable of liberating people from the bland roles and assumptions they've accepted in our B-movie society of the spectacle, *Avant-Pop* announces that reports about the death of a literary avant-garde have been greatly exaggerated.

Larry McCaffery's most recent books include *Storming the*

Reality Studio: A Casebook of Cyberpunk and Postmodern SF and *Across the Wounded Galaxies: Interviews with Contemporary American SF Writers.*
Paper, ISBN: 0-932511-72-44, $7.00

New Noir

Stories by John Shirley

In *New Noir*, John Shirley, like a postmodern Edgar Allen Poe, depicts minds deformed into fantastic configurations by the pressure, the very weight, of an entire society bearing down on them. "Jody and Annie on TV," selected by the editor of *Mystery Scene* as "perhaps the most important story...in years in the crime fiction genre," reflects the fact that whole segments of zeitgeist and personal psychology have been supplanted by the mass media, that the average kid on the streets in Los Angeles is in a radical crisis of exploded self-image, and that life really is meaningless for millions. The stories here also bring to mind Elmore Leonard and the better crime novelists, but John Shirley—unlike writers who attempt to extrapolate from peripheral observation and research—bases his stories on his personal experience of extreme people and extreme mental states, and his struggle with the seductions of drugs, crime, prostitution, and violence.

John Shirley has been a lead singer in a rock bank, Obsession, writes lyrics for various bands, including Blue Oyster Cult, and in his spare time records with the Panther Moderns. He is the author of numerous works in a variety of genres; his story collection *Heatseeker* was chosen by the Locus Reader's Poll as one of the best collections of 1989. His latest novel is *Wetbones*.

"John Shirley serves up the bloody heart of a rotting society with the aplomb of an Aztec surgeon on Dexedrine."

—***ALA Booklist***

Paper, ISBN: 0-932511-55-4, $7.00

The Ethiopian Exhibition
A novel by D.N. Stuefloten
While World War II rages in Europe, John Twelve climbs onto a four-cylinder Indian motorcycle and crosses Ethiopia, searching for truth, for beauty, for mystery. At the same time, a modern American girl strolls the streets of Puerto Vallarta, where she is accosted by a film director—actually Ahmed, an Ethiopian murderer. He is making a film, he explains, about a man crossing the Ethiopian desert on a motorcycle. The girl accepts a starring role—and with this embarks on an adventure that takes her beyond the limits of ordinary reality. Her companions on this mystery tour include Sheba, the 3,000-year-old Queen of Ethiopia; Prester John, the legendary King of Ethiopia; and the Emperor Haile Selassie, the Conquering Lion of Judah. The innocent American girl, now called Dominique, watches in amazement and alarm as the world reveals an esoteric reality that she never knew existed.

D.N. Stuefloten has spent most of his life wandering around the world writing novels. He has been a magician's assistant in Africa, the manager of a mining company in Borneo, a fisherman in the south seas, and a smuggler in India. His first novel, *Maya,* was published in 1992 by Fiction Collective Two.
Paper, ISBN: 0-932511-85-6, $7.00

Individuals may order any or all of the Black Ice Book series directly from Fiction Collective Two, Publication Unit, Illinois State University, Campus Box 4241, Normal, IL 61790-4241. (Check or money order only, made payable to Fiction Collective Two.) Bookstore, library, and text orders must be placed through the distributor: The Talman Company, Inc., 131 Spring Street, #201 E-N, New York, NY 10012; Customer Service: 800/537-8894.